Beyond the Shadows

Beyond
the
Shadows

by
SALLIE LEE BELL

ZONDERVAN PUBLISHING HOUSE
GRAND RAPIDS, MICHIGAN

Printed in the United States of America

CHAPTER 1

LISA CAME OUT INTO THE WARM SPRING MORNING to dry
her hair. The shimmering blackness of it glistened in the
sunlight as it curled in wet tendrils about her lovely face.
She ran her fingers through it and shook it out. It rested
in a black cloud about the smooth skin of her face, making
it lighter by contrast.

Her dark eyes under the arched brows were large and
brilliant. They reflected her changing moods, glowing and
tender or flashing with anger, or sometimes misted with
tears. Her features gave no hint of her nationality. She
could have been taken for a Spanish beauty or a native of
Italy, though she had been born where her father had been
born and where she lived, in a little German town near
the border of France.

As she lifted her eyes to the far distant mountains,
a dreamy light crept into them. Some day, perhaps, she
would cross those mountains to the sea. She and Paul would
sail to America, that dreamland of prosperity and liberty,
where there was no shadow of fear from a ruler who seemed
to grow more violent as time went by.

As the thought of that dream swept through her mind,
her eyes glowed with a tender light that softened their
brilliance. But this was her dream, not Paul's, or, if it was,
he had never mentioned it. They spent many hours during
their school years talking of a future that they felt that they
would spend together, even when they were only children.
They had lived across the street from each other all their
lives and their families had been friends, so it was natural

that she and Paul should play together and be companionable when they grew older.

Though Paul was all boy, he was gentle and thoughtful of her, even as a little fellow. He loved sports but he was also quiet and studious. He loved to read, and often when their lessons were finished they would sit outside under the big tree or, in the winter time, before the fireplace, while Paul read fairy stories to her and later, stories of adventure.

When they finished high school, Paul went to work in a shop and Lisa learned to sew and cook and keep house. They still dreamed of the future and Lisa still dreamed of America. They had studied English and they both spoke it fluently, Lisa with scarcely an accent. Though Paul had never spoken to her of love, she took it for granted that some day they would be married.

Paul had never told her that he loved her because, as they grew older, there was Hans who seemed to be coming between them, Hans who hovered around Lisa as a bee hovers around a lovely flower. It made Paul angry and jealousy surged within him, but he kept his love locked within his heart, fearful that if he told Lisa of his love, she might tell him that she loved Hans. It had been a shock when he realized how completely Hans had come between them.

Since Hans came from a wealthy home, he had no need to work long hours as Paul did. Often when Paul came home and ate a hurried meal so that he could be with Lisa, he would find Hans already there and Lisa seemed to be enjoying his company more than she had ever enjoyed being with him. It hurt him and he was disappointed in Lisa. He had thought, ever since he could remember, that she belonged to him. Now he felt that he was losing her, if he hadn't already lost her.

Lisa had no idea of how Paul felt or how hurt he was, though she wondered why he had changed. She began to fear that he was no longer interested in her. She had been sure of his love. She tried to make him jealous by pretending to be interested in Hans. She didn't know that, instead of rousing his jealousy, she was driving him from her.

This morning, as she stood in the sunlight gazing at the distant mountains, there was nothing but happiness in her heart, the happiness that her dreams brought her. She must tell Paul some day soon what her dreams were and find out whether he could dream with her about America. Of course, if he still cared for her and if he didn't want to go, she would be satisfied to stay here. She would be satisfied anywhere, just so she was with him.

Life had been good to Lisa and she had never known care or privation. Her father, Nathaniel Bergen, had a shop in town and was fairly prosperous. Life had always been peaceful and uneventful, but happy.

Lately there had appeared upon the horizon of their lives a small cloud. Hitler had come into power and he was beginning to show his real aim in life. He had dreams also, dreams of being the ruler of the world. As yet the cloud was tiny and there seemed no cause for worry, but sometimes Nathaniel wondered what would happen if Hitler should really undertake world conquest. Nathaniel was steeped in the history of his people and he knew how many times they had been the special object of cruelty and persecution through the centuries.

Somewhere within there lurked a small fear at times, that once more his people might be the object of persecution and suffering. When he read the papers and this fear rose within him, he thrust it aside and refused to let his thoughts dwell upon it. He had faith in Jehovah God. He trusted that God would protect them from any further persecutions, even if war should come. Just now there seemed no immediate cause for worry, so he never spoke of how he felt, even to his wife.

Nathaniel's wife, Elizabeth, had the features which Lisa had inherited, and which revealed that somewhere in the line of her ancestors, someone had married outside of his faith. Her black eyes, short straight nose and full red lips betrayed Castilian blood. Lisa bore her mother's name, though no one ever called her Elizabeth.

Elizabeth, with her husband, was faithful to the religion which had been handed down to them through the ages. They kept the feast days, and observed the Passover with what was left of the ancient and solemn ritual. They observed the Day of Atonement, though there was no synagogue in the town. Nathaniel and his near neighbors of the same faith met in one or other of their houses for a day of prayer and meditation. That was the extent of their religious life and, except for faith in the God of Abraham, Isaac and Jacob, there was no hope in Nathaniel's heart of a better life in the future. He was living solely in the present, happy and content with his life with his family and friends.

Lisa began to sing a little song as she shook her hair out and waited for it to dry. She was going to a party that night and she was always excited at the prospect of a party. There would be games and dancing and she would be wearing her new dress which she knew was becoming.

There was only one little blot on the picture as she thought of the party. She would be going with Hans and she had wanted to go with Paul. She had hoped that Paul would ask her, but Hans had asked first and she couldn't refuse him without a good excuse. She wondered if Paul would ask her. A few months ago she would have been sure, but now she wasn't. Whenever Paul came over, he was moody and silent and their close relationship seemed to have disappeared. They used to find much to talk about, but now there seemed little to say. If she asked him about his work he answered in monosyllables. When they sat out under the tree, sometimes she would ask him to read to her, hoping that this would make him more cheerful. She had a book which she knew he would enjoy, but he told her that he wasn't in the mood for reading.

His indifference hurt her deeply. Panic seized her when she thought that perhaps he had found someone else and that he no longer cared for her at all. What would life be without him? He had been a part of her every waking hour and often the center of her dreams. He had always been the center of her daydreams. His infrequent visits became more painful than pleasant for both of them.

She had no idea of what was going on in Paul's mind and how heavy his heart was. She didn't know that Paul stayed away because the very fact of her nearness and fear that she no longer cared, brought such pain that he no longer enjoyed being with her. Better to think of her and long for her than to be with her and try to overcome the desire to take her in his arms and tell her of his love, to tell her that neither Hans or anyone should take her from him. That would only cause her unhappiness if she should have to tell him that she was in love with Hans.

When he had been invited to the party at Elsa's home, he hesitated to ask Lisa to go with him, for he felt that she would rather go with Hans, but he finally determined that he would ask her and find out the worst. When he asked her, she looked at him solemnly and told him that Hans had asked her and that she was going with him.

"I expected that," he said dejectedly. "I shouldn't have asked you."

"Why do you say that?" she asked.

"I should have known that you would want to go with him."

"But I don't!" she burst out. "I was hoping that you would ask me. Why did you wait so long?"

"Because I believed that you were in love with him," he said as his sorrowful eyes met her gaze.

Her eyes rested pensively upon him for a moment, taking in every loved feature, the dark wavy hair, the high-bridged nose, the straight, level brows, the firm chin and the dark eyes that could be so tender and which now seemed so remote and lusterless. He was handsome and her heart beat faster as she looked at him.

"You're a very stupid person," she remarked as she left him and went into the house.

He stood there perplexed by her sudden anger and by what she had said. What she had said gave him hope. She said that she'd rather go with him. But her sudden anger and her abrupt departure dropped him again into the depths of woe. Girls were strange creatures, he mused, as he left the house and returned home. He had had no difficulty in understanding Lisa when they were children, but now that she was no longer a child, she became a puzzle.

He decided that he wouldn't go to the party. He wouldn't enjoy being there and seeing Lisa and Hans. But then, in a sudden spurt of rebellion against his own state of mind, he decided that he would go. He'd ask Greda to go with him. Greda wasn't pretty, but she was jolly and she had a good personality. They were old friends and he liked her. He might not have such a dull time if he went with her.

Perhaps Lisa would be jealous if she saw him with another girl. He had never dated any other girl and this would be a surprise to her, even if she wasn't jealous. He wondered how she could be so interested in Hans. He wasn't of her faith. Hans was all German and he thought Hitler was the greatest leader in the world. How could Lisa's father allow Hans to show so much interest in Lisa?

The more he thought about Lisa and Hans, the more gloomy he became and he had about decided that, after all, he wouldn't go to the party, but just as he reached the gate of his home he saw Greda coming toward him. She waved to him. Her bright smile warmed his heart and he felt more cheerful as he waited for her to come nearer.

"I was just thinking of asking you if you would go with me to the party," he told her.

"It must have taken you a long time to think over this important matter," she said with a broad grin. "Otherwise you would have asked me sooner. This surely is a last minute request."

"I'm a slow thinker," he responded with a smile. "Even if I am late, will you allow me to take you, if you're not already spoken for? I'd like to, very much."

"I know I'm second choice," she said, "but it just so happens that no one else has asked me, so I'll accept your offer. I'll be happy to go with you." Then in more serious vein, "What's happened between you and Lisa? Has someone else beat you to it and left you out in the cold? I know you'd rather go with her, so be honest and tell me the truth. You know that I know you, Paul." This time her smile was kind and sympathetic. "I know there is only one girl in your life. You've never made any secret of that. Has old foxy Hans beat your time?"

"As I said, I'm a slow thinker," he replied with a faint smile. "I just waited too long to ask her. But I'm sure we can have fun together."

"You'd better watch that Hans fellow," Greda warned. "He's in love with your girl and he's a stubborn person. I'd hate to make him my enemy. He's as vindictive as he is stubborn."

"He's not a Jew," Paul remarked seriously. "I can't understand why Lisa should be so interested in him."

"Those things don't seem to matter too much any more," Greda remarked. "That's the way it should be, shouldn't it? We mingle together here without any thought in our group about religion. We've learned that it doesn't matter too much one way or another. We're living for the present and we can't bother too much about rituals and religion. All we want is freedom to have fun while we're young."

"It's not that way with the Jews," Paul said gravely. "We're still faithful to the traditions of our ancestors, though I'll confess that I can't see what good it has ever brought us. Our people have been hunted down and persecuted for centuries just because we are true to our traditions. I'm glad that Lisa and I are accepted by the rest of you and I've always appreciated your friendship."

"How did we get started on this track?" Greda asked. "What do I care what your religious beliefs are? I'm glad you asked me to go with you, Paul, for if you hadn't, I suppose I would have stayed at home and missed all the fun. I'll try not to be a bore and if I can get that foxy Hans away from Lisa long enough to give you a chance, I'll do my best to keep him away."

"Thanks, but don't bother about Hans," he answered.

"We'll forget him and have fun. I'll call for you on time, I promise."

What was the matter with Lisa, Greda wondered as she continued on her way. How could she be so foolish as to turn down such a wonderful person as Paul for someone like Hans? The only redeeming thing about Hans was that he had money while Paul had nothing. But when it came to love, money shouldn't matter. She'd take Paul herself, if he would have her, money or no money. She had loved him as long as she could remember, when they were children playing together, getting dirty playing in mud, going on little picnics and getting stung by bees. But always it had been Lisa, and Greda accepted it without bitterness.

When they grew older and were in school together, Lisa accepted Paul's devotion with such indifference that sometimes it made Greda angry. Just one smile from Paul and one slight caress when they played together, set Greda's heart pounding and joy racing through her. She would have given anything she possessed or ever hoped to have, if she could possess what Lisa had. But now they were grown and there seemed to have come a rift between these two. Perhaps Paul might turn to her one day as he had this afternoon. She didn't want to hope, for she didn't want to be disloyal to her friend, but she couldn't help but wish that Lisa would continue to let Hans pay her attention. It would hurt Paul and she would hate to have him hurt, but perhaps the hurt might be healed and he might learn to care just a little for her.

She couldn't wipe that thought from her mind and when she dressed for the party, she took more care than usual to make herself as attractive as possible for Paul. As she surveyed herself in the mirror, she was forced to admit that she presented no image of ravishing beauty. Her mouth was too large and her nose wasn't long enough. She had the high cheek bones which were characteristic of her German origin.

She shrugged her shoulders and her heart sank a little as she turned away from the mirror. Paul's heart would never quicken with admiration of her, even though she did look more attractive than usual.

She was glad that tonight Lisa had turned him down. She would take every little crumb of happiness that came her way from him. Her face was radiant as she greeted him and they went off together for the party which was just a few blocks away.

CHAPTER 2

LISA TRIED TO CONVINCE HERSELF that she was happy as she waited for Hans to arrive, but she knew that she wasn't. She couldn't forget the look of defeat and disappointment on Paul's face and the hurt look in his eyes when she told him that she was going with Hans. She knew that she would have been excited if she had been waiting for Paul. She knew that the joy which she had been anticipating was disappearing and she wondered if, after all, she would have a good time.

Perhaps Paul wouldn't come and if he wasn't there, no matter how many others might hover around her, there would be no thrill in it. Even if Paul came, he might not even ask her for a dance.

Her musings were interrupted by the arrival of Hans. When she let him in he stood for a moment staring at her in admiration.

"You look beautiful tonight!" he exclaimed.

She was beautiful, for the dress with its bouffant skirt and tight bodice was becoming. The fresh beauty of youth glowed in her lovely eyes and upon her cheeks, while the dark mass of her curly hair framed her face in shining ringlets.

"Thank you," she murmured as they went out into the darkness and walked the short distance to the house where the party was to be held.

There were a number of others there when they arrived and the girls greeted Lisa with exclamations, telling her how pretty she looked. The boys had no words, but there

14

was no need for words. Their eyes and the way they gathered around her told her more than mere words could have done.

She looked around eagerly for Paul but she didn't see him and her heart sank a little, for she had hoped he would be there and that he would see that others liked her even if he ceased to care. Presently he came and she tried to conceal her surprise when she saw that he was with Greda. Their entrance caused a small sensation for many in the group knew that he had never dated anyone but Lisa. There was a moment's silence while the hostess greeted them.

One of the girls turned to Lisa and whispered, "What's the matter? Have you and Paul had a quarrel?"

"No," Lisa replied as calmly as possible, for her heart was pounding and there was a strange little pain that accompanied that pounding. Greda's eyes were glowing and Lisa admitted that she looked better than she had ever looked before. Happiness beamed from her eyes and shone upon her face.

"Then what's happened?" the girl persisted in a whisper to Lisa. "Have you let Greda beat your time with Paul?"

Lisa turned upon her with an amused smile. At least she hoped the smile appeared amused. She felt that it was a poor shadow of a smile, for her heart wasn't smiling at all.

"No, silly, of course not," she said. "He asked me for a date, but Hans had already asked me. So I guess he asked Greda."

There was at least a small satisfaction in that fact. He had asked her first.

"I wonder if Greda knows she was second choice."

"I'm sure I don't know, nor do I care," Lisa replied as she turned away.

That wasn't true and she knew it wasn't. She hoped that Greda did know that she was second choice. She hoped that she wouldn't dislike Greda for being with Paul tonight, for she and Greda had always been good friends, but she felt jealousy rising within her and she didn't like that sensation. She had never known it before.

She couldn't be happy when Paul danced with her, for he had little to say and she was almost glad when the dance was over. She tried to appear friendly with Greda and she hoped that Greda wouldn't guess what was in her heart toward her tonight.

She tried to hide that little ache in her heart by being even more gay and talkative than usual. She had always been popular and tonight, if she had been vain, her vanity would have been satisfied, for she was the center of an admiring group whenever there was a lull in the festivities. But though she glowed, she wasn't happy. Her eyes would often wander to Paul and Greda. They were a little apart from the group surrounding her. Paul seemed to be doing his best to keep her entertained and if she missed the attention of the other boys, she didn't seem to mind.

Paul wondered if she did and if she was hurt because few of them paid her more than casual attention. He felt embarrassed for her, but he need not have been. She knew that she wasn't attractive. The boys liked her and they let it go at that. She was a good pal at school and a good friend after school days were over, but nothing more. But she was with Paul tonight and nothing else mattered. She would ask for nothing more if she only had him, but she felt that this would never be. She was his tonight because Lisa was with Hans. She didn't care if she was second choice. She was happy tonight, even if Paul had rather be with Lisa.

Just before the party was over Paul danced with Lisa again.

"You're lovely tonight," he remarked as he looked at her with her face so close to his. "But then you always are. You always have been to me, even when you were a tiny little thing all covered with mud."

She gave him a warm smile as she said, "That's the nicest thing I've heard all evening."

"There are many here like Hans who would try to take you from me," he said as the hurt look returned to his eyes.

"Trying doesn't always mean succeeding," she told him with a flash of her dark eyes and the hint of coquetry in her smile.

She longed to tell him that no one could ever take his place, no matter how hard they might try, but she decided that if he was that easily discouraged, she'd let him suffer for a while. If he saw that there were others, he might not think too seriously about Hans. It was good to know that he hadn't changed. He was jealous. Now she knew, for she had recently felt that same cruel little pang. It was there no longer and she felt that she could like Greda again. She felt sorry for Greda, for she was sure that Greda liked Paul. Who wouldn't? But Greda could never have him. He was all hers. He always would be. She'd never let anyone take him from her.

When the dance was finished she went over to Greda and talked to her. She had scarcely spoken to her all evening. She couldn't be a hypocrite and pretend something she didn't feel, but now it was different.

"I hope you've had a good time," she remarked. "It's been a lovely party, hasn't it?"

"I've had a wonderful time," Greda replied. "It's the nicest party I've ever been to."

Her eyes glowed and there was a happy smile upon her lips. She saw Paul coming toward them and he was looking at her and not at Lisa.

"Greda says that this is the best party she's ever attended," Lisa told him. "I agree with her. It's been a lovely evening and I've had loads of fun."

"You should have, the way the boys swarmed around you," Greda remarked. "I don't blame them," she conceded good naturedly. "You're the prettiest one here tonight. If I were a boy, I'd have been right there, too."

Lisa laughed. "Thanks for the compliment, but I'm glad you're not a boy. I'd rather have you for my friend, just as you are. Do come over soon. I haven't seen much of you since you went to work."

"I'll do that," Greda told her.

They parted as Hans approached and soon afterwards they left and walked toward their homes. Lisa could see Paul and Greda just a little way ahead of them. She wished with all her heart that it were she clinging to Paul's arm so possessively, instead of Greda.

CHAPTER 3

NATHANIEL HAD OBSERVED THE GROWING INTIMACY between Lisa and Hans and he wondered what he should do about it. He had never liked the boy, even as a little fellow, although he couldn't place his finger upon anything definite that caused his dislike. He had sometimes watched them in their play and he observed that Hans always managed to get what he wanted and to have his way whenever there was an argument as to who should be first in some game. He was ruthless, even though he had a certain charm. But there was some underlying trait that made Nathaniel distrust him as a young man.

Nathaniel and Hans' father, Herr Bauer, had been friends for many years and while the children were young, his dislike of the boy did not influence him to prevent them from playing together. Now he saw with growing concern Lisa's apparent interest in Hans. The thought of marriage between them was abhorrent for several reasons. They were not of the same faith and that, to Nathaniel, was important. Though he was forced to acknowledge to himself that his religious belief had never brought him peace or joy or hope, still, the ingrained laws of his forefathers persisted with him. His daughter must marry within the confines of her own race and with someone of her own belief.

He had always thought of Paul as the one Lisa would marry and that thought pleased him. Paul was a fine young man and though he had nothing but his small salary, he had intelligence and was a hard worker and Nathaniel felt that some day before long he would be well able to support a wife.

Until recently he had no doubt that these two would be married. Perhaps one day they would all be able to move to America where there was peace and liberty, with no shadow of fear looming upon any horizon. There would be equal opportunity for all, no matter what their race or creed might be. He had had this dream for a long time, though he had never mentioned it to his wife. There would be time enough for that when the dream would be nearer fulfillment.

Lately, when the shadow of Hitler was becoming more threatening, this dream became a longing, but he knew that at present there seemed little hope of it ever being realized. Now the matter of Hans was becoming a problem which must be dealt with before it was too late.

The morning after the party Nathaniel told Lisa that he wanted to talk to her. He led the way into the living room while Elizabeth went into the kitchen. She wondered what her father wanted. Whenever he had had a talk with her before, which he sometimes did to reprimand her for something she had done, her mother was always there.

"What's wrong, Papa?" she asked when he closed the door and faced her with serious eyes.

"It's about Hans," he said.

"About Hans," she repeated, staring at him in surprise. "What has he done?"

He smiled faintly. "It isn't what he has done, it's what I fear he may do. He's been so attentive lately that he's taken up practically all of your time. I scarcely ever see Paul around any more. I don't like that, Lisa."

"Why not? I thought you liked Hans."

"I don't," he declared. "I never have liked him. There is something about him that makes me dislike him, though I confess that I can't say what it is. He's the kind of fellow who will do anything to get what he wants, no matter who it hurts. And right now it looks as if he wants you."

"He has been coming around a lot lately," she admitted. "But I didn't know you'd mind."

"What have you done to Paul to make him stay away?

I thought you two were inseparable. I always thought you'd marry him one day. What's come between you? Hans?"

"I think Paul is angry because Hans comes here so often."

"He's angry because he loves you, Lisa. He thinks you care for Hans and he's staying away because he's hurt."

"If he's not man enough to fight for what he wants, then let him stay away," she said with a toss of her head. "If he loves me, then why doesn't he do something about it besides pouting and sulking?"

"Because he's not the kind of boy that Hans is," her father told her. "If he thinks you prefer Hans, he's willing to let you have what you want and not make you unhappy by interfering. I think that's noble of him."

"It may be noble, but I'd rather see him a little more like Hans. He gives up too easily."

"Do you love Hans?" her father asked while he looked at her seriously and anxiously.

She gave him a smile, then went to him and patted him upon his cheek.

"Don't worry, Papa dear. I'm not in the least in love with Hans. He's good company and he does try to please me in every way, but I could never love him."

"Then is it Paul?" he asked hopefully with a relieved sigh.

"It will always be Paul," she said.

"Then don't run the risk of losing him by flirting with Hans," he admonished. "It isn't right and it may bring you sorrow. Hans is not a Jew. And he's ruthless and vindictive. Don't lead him on or you may regret it."

"What harm could Hans do to me?" she asked skeptically.

"Perhaps nothing. I just don't know. But I want you to be on the safe side, so don't take any chances."

"You talk as if you're afraid of something. What's the matter, Papa? I've noticed lately that you seem worried about something. That's not like you. What is it?"

"I am worried," he admitted reluctantly, "though I've not wanted to talk about it. I don't like the looks of things in Berlin. Herr Hitler has been making speeches and I don't like the sound of them. He talks about liberating enslaved people of other countries like Poland and Czechoslovakia, but I know that there is something in his mind that gives the lie to his speeches. I fear that he is inciting the people to war. If war comes, Lisa, our people may suffer. It has been that way often and I fear that it will always be, unless our Messiah should come to liberate us."

"I wonder if that will ever happen. I wonder if there really is a Messiah," she added. "Even if there is such a person, what good is it to hope for anything from Him in our lifetime? Why not renounce our faith and be free from fear, Papa? What good does it do to us to be true to our religion, when it means nothing to us?"

"That's a terrible thing you're saying, Lisa," he said sternly. "Don't ever say it again. Renouncing our religion wouldn't change us. We're Jews and we shall always be Jews. Our God made us so, and all through the centuries we have been a separate people, not because we wanted to be, but because He has made us so. Renouncing our religion would never save us from persecution, for, no matter what we might believe, in the eyes of the world we would still be Jews and we would suffer as such."

"It seems to me that God has put a curse upon us," she said bitterly. "We call ourselves the chosen people of God, yet He allows us to be driven from country to country and endure persecution and suffering from Gentiles whom we despise, or at least we're supposed to. Why is this, if we're the chosen people? Why should we have to be afraid if war should come? Why doesn't God protect His own?"

"I can't answer that, my child," Nathaniel said sadly. "I only know that war has often given the Gentiles an excuse to plunder and rob our people. If war should come, Hitler will need no excuse to do the same with us. He will need money and our people have much."

"What good is that, if it's always taken from us? Perhaps I would do well to marry Hans," she said flippantly. "Then I'd be safe, for he would protect me. I would no longer be a despised Jew. I'd be the wife of a wealthy German, one whose father is a friend of one of Hitler's officers."

"Now you're talking nonsense," he retorted. "Would you marry for your own safety and leave your parents to suffer at the hands of their enemies?"

"Of course not, Papa. You know that. I was only joking. Let's not think of such gloomy things as war and persecution. I want to live and be happy, and if prayers are any good, I shall pray that we may live out our lives and forget that we might be under the shadow of suffering."

"Then send Hans on his way, but try to keep him as your friend," he advised anxiously.

"I can't send him on his way unless there is some reason why I should. He's never mentioned love to me. He's just been a friend. As long as he is just that, I'll try to keep him just a friend. And I will try to be more friendly to Paul and not be angry with him, if that is what you want."

"Isn't that what you want?" he asked as he put an arm around her and lifted her face to his.

"Yes, but he's made me angry by sulking. He's almost made me believe that he didn't care any longer."

He kissed her and left for town while she went into the kitchen to help her mother. He was relieved about Hans, but his worry over the political situation remained with him. He had read the fiery speeches of Hitler and he had heard rumors from customers in the shop. It looked as if war was drawing nearer. He could only hope that his fears were groundless and that if war should come, it would be in the far distant future. Perhaps before then they might get to America and be out of it all.

A few evenings later Hans came. He and Lisa sat out under the tree. Presently Hans took hold of her hand and tried to draw her closer. She resisted his effort though she let him hold her hand.

"Don't pull away from me, Lisa," he begged. "I've been

wanting to tell you what was in my heart for a long time
and I can't wait any longer. I love you, Lisa. I'm sure you've
known it, because I didn't try to hide it. I've loved you ever
since we were children. I want you to marry me, Lisa.
You will, won't you?"

She was nettled by his self confidence. He seemed
to have no doubts that she would refuse him.

"You wouldn't want me to marry you if I didn't love
you, would you?" she asked.

"I'd want you any way that I could get you," he asserted.
"But you do love me, don't you? I was sure that you did."

"I'm sorry if you felt that way, Hans, but I don't. I
like you and we've had a lot of fun together, but I don't
love you. I'm sorry if that hurts you, but I have to be
honest with you."

"Then why have you kept me dangling around all this
time, if you didn't love me?" he asked angrily. "Just trying
to make a fool of me?"

"Of course not!" she cried indignantly. "I never kept
you dangling. I never even thought of it that way. You
came around often and I was glad that you came, for I like
you as I told you, and we had fun together. Couldn't I do
that without making a fool of you? I never thought of such
a thing."

"I suppose you're in love with Paul," he remarked
bitterly.

"I didn't say that I was in love with anyone," she replied.

"You don't have to say it. I know he's always hung
around you ever since we were children, but I didn't think
you cared for him. Now I hate him more than ever, if he's
stolen you from me."

"You shouldn't talk that way, Hans," she remonstrated.
"Paul hasn't stolen me from you. I just don't love you. I
like you as my friend and I shall always want you for my
friend, but I can't marry you. Please don't be angry because I can't."

He stared at her gloomily and didn't answer.

"I'm sure your father wouldn't want me for your wife, for we are of different races and different religions," she told him.

"My father will have nothing to say about the girl I marry," he stated emphatically. He turned upon her angrily. "You should feel flattered because I love you. I should despise you as many of my people do, because you're a Jew. You should feel honored because I offer you marriage. Many of my people would think that I had degraded myself by marrying a Jew."

"If that's the way you feel, then I'm fortunate that I don't love you," she said coldly. Then she raised her head and looked at him with eyes that flashed with fire. "You have the situation reversed, Hans. That's exactly the way my people regard all Gentiles. They would think that I had degraded myself if I married you. My people are the chosen of God and that is something to be proud of."

He laughed harshly. "Chosen of God! What has that ever got you? Nothing that I can see."

"We have a heritage that we can be proud of. We are the descendants of Abraham who was called the friend of God and to whom God gave many promises. We are a separate and a pure race. What do your people have to boast of? They're a mixture of all the savage tribes that invaded your land from time to time through the centuries. You have nothing to boast of, so don't think that you should despise me. I might be tempted to feel the same way about you."

He stared at her in surprise. He had never seen her like this. In all their years together they had never discussed their differences. The few Jewish families in town had mingled with their neighbors and had been accepted by them. It had been that way with the two families living near Hans, Paul's family and Lisa's.

"I didn't mean to say that and I'm sorry," Hans admitted contritely. "Can't you give me a little hope, Lisa? I'm willing to wait and keep on hoping, if you'll tell me that I can."

"Please don't put it that way, Hans," she begged. "Just let me be your friend. My father would never want us to marry, even if I loved you. He wants me to marry in my own faith."

"Your father might need my friendship if war should come," Hans remarked. "Refusing me as a son-in-law surely wouldn't help him if he ever needed my friendship."

"What do you mean by that?" she asked. "You can't hold my father to blame because I don't love you."

"Forget it," he said. "I didn't really mean anything. But if war should come, there's no telling what may happen. I'd want to protect you from any harm that might threaten you. I'm a pretty stubborn person, as you ought to know. I don't give up easily and what I want, I usually get. Don't forget that."

He took her suddenly in his arms and kissed her swiftly and passionately, though she struggled to free herself. He held her to him while he laughed a low, teasing laugh.

"It's no use to struggle," he said, with his face close to hers. "It won't do you any good to struggle against me and the love I have for you. I'll win you, see if I don't."

He let her go and she wiped her mouth as if the touch of his lips had defiled them.

He bent over her and whispered, "Don't ever forget that kiss, Lisa. It tells you that you belong to me."

He was gone without giving her the chance to reply. She was so angry that she couldn't have replied if he had waited. Beneath the anger and humiliation there lurked a little fear. She remembered his hint of a threat to her father. She knew that if war should come, Hans might be in a position to harm her father if he wanted to, for she remembered that Hans' father had friends in Berlin and Hans might be in a position to fulfill any threat he might have made.

She remembered her recent conversation with her father and as she went into the house, the small fear persisted, though she tried to forget it. It remained to haunt her in her dreams.

CHAPTER 4

WHEN NATHANIEL CAME HOME the next evening Lisa told him what had happened between Hans and herself. She was disappointed at his reaction. Instead of the feeling of relief she had expected, his face was grave and his voice was serious.

"I'm glad that that's settled," he said. "That takes a weight off my mind, but I'm afraid he won't give you up easily. If he really loves you, he'll do everything in his power to get you. He's that kind of fellow."

"He can't make me marry him against my will and I made him understand that he'd just as well forget that he loves me."

"I know, but I also know Hans. If times were different, I wouldn't be worried, but we're on the border of dangerous times, my child, and we don't know what may happen in the future. Hans' love for you may turn to hate. Then he might take revenge by hurting you through someone else someone whom you might love dearly."

"You mean he would try to harm you or Mama?" she asked with wide eyes.

"Or Paul."

"Oh, I don't think he's that mean. I know he's stubborn and he always tries to get what he wants, but what could he do to harm any of you three? I don't think he's that low."

"We don't know how mean a person can become in these times," he persisted. "Hitler's men have organized the Hitler Youth in Berlin and other cities. I've heard that they're extending all over the country. Someone in the store today was talking about this movement. It's a dangerous and unholy thing. These young people are taught to look upon Hitler as their God and they are taught to be informers and the very opposite of what God-fearing parents would teach them. They are taught cruelty."

"I'm sure that Hans doesn't belong to anything like that," she said. "I don't think he even knows anything about such an organization."

"I'm not so sure of that," her father replied. "I remember now that only a few days ago I saw a soldier ride in. I thought nothing of it at the time. He was driving an officer of the army and they stopped at Herr Bauer's. I saw the car parked there when I came home that evening. He may have been here for the same purpose as this man talked about in the store. I know that Herr Bauer has connections with some of Hitler's council. I never thought much about it until recently. I'm beginning to wonder whom we can trust. The future is beginning to look darker, Lisa, and I confess that I'm worried. I hadn't meant to say all of this, but you might as well know and be prepared, for none of us can tell what may come."

"This does look bad," Lisa murmured. "Let's hope that nothing will come of it. Life is so full of happiness. I do hope that nothing comes up to bring suffering to any of us."

For a while her father's words weighed heavily upon her, but when she saw no signs of what he seemed to fear and as life went on as usual, she, with the resilience of youth, shook off the weight and the memory of it and continued to enjoy life as she found it.

Hans stayed away and she was glad of that. She hoped that Paul would come over soon and life would go on as it had before Hans became such a regular visitor. She was disappointed, however, for he didn't come and the fear grew that, after all, she had lost him. She saw him coming home from work each evening, for she watched for him, hoping that he would come over.

She decided that she would go to see Greda and see if

she could find out anything about what Paul was doing. She went over one evening.

"You wouldn't come to see me, so I thought I'd come and see you," she explained as Greda let her in.

"Since I'm working, I don't have much time for anything else," Greda explained.

"How do you like your work?" Lisa asked.

"I don't like anything except the money I make," Greda said. "I've decided to save every penny that I can so that perhaps one day I can go to America. Perhaps I'll find a rich husband over there, one who won't mind that I'm not beautiful," she added with a laugh.

"I've always dreamed of going to America one day," Lisa told her. "They say that it's a wonderful country. A land of wonderful opportunity. But that dream may never come true."

"You surely don't have to go that far to find a husband," Greda said with a mischievous twinkle in her eyes. "Not with two of the most eligible boys in town in love with you."

"And who might they be?" Lisa asked.

"As if you didn't know. Hans and Paul, of course."

"Thanks for telling me," Lisa said with a smile. Her heart seemed suddenly lighter. "Since I can't marry both of them, which one would you recommend as a husband?"

"You know which one," Greda replied. "I'd hate to think you'd prefer Hans. He's a Nazi through and through and I don't trust one of them. Paul loves you and you know it. He'd make you as happy as any girl could ever want to be. I'd give anything in the world if I had someone like him."

"I hope you find that someone some day," Lisa said gently. "You deserve the best."

"We don't always get what we deserve, though, do we? Let's have a cup of coffee. Now that I've given you some good advice, we can talk about something else. How about that new picture? Have you seen it?"

Lisa said that she hadn't.

"Then let's go tomorrow night. That is, if you don't have a date."

"I don't and I'd be glad to go."

"Then I'll be by for you right after supper," Greda suggested.

When Lisa left she hummed a little song as she walked along. Her heart was light again. Paul loved her. He hadn't been interested in Greda at least.

Later that evening as they sat at supper, Lisa was so bubbling over with joy that her parents wondered what had brought about the sudden change. Lately she had not seemed as happy as she should have been.

"Something wonderful must have happened to make you so happy," her mother remarked. "I haven't seen you like this for a long time. What's happened?"

"Nothing in particular," Lisa told her. "I'm just happy, that's all. Greda and I had a nice visit together and we're going to the show tomorrow night, if it's all right with you."

"Are you two old maids going alone?" her father asked with a smile. He was glad that her sudden joy had nothing to do with Hans.

"Yes, since no one has been thoughtful enough to ask to take us," she replied. "But it's good for us girls to get together once in a while. We don't often get the chance."

"At least *you* don't," her mother said. "It's good to see that Hans doesn't hang around so much these last few days. What have you done to him?"

Lisa realized that she hadn't told her mother what had happened between Hans and herself.

"I told him that we'd better be just friends, so he stayed away," she explained.

"That's good news," her mother said in relieved tones. "But how about Paul? What have you done to him? His mother told me today that he sits around the house and mopes as if he'd lost his last friend."

"I haven't done anything to him," Lisa said while her heart beat happily. "It'll do him good to sit and mope for a while. He'll snap out of it some day, I'm sure."

When she and Greda left for the movie, she saw a light in Paul's room. He was at home, perhaps moping, as his mother had said. She wished she could call to him as she had done when they were children and invite him to come out and go with them.

The theater was already filling when they arrived and they followed the crowd inside. The picture was not too interesting and Lisa was glad when it was over.

"That surely was a flop," Greda remarked as they came out. "It was a waste of time and money."

"I've enjoyed being with you," Lisa replied. "It seemed like old times."

"Look who I see," Greda said as they turned toward home.

Paul was standing in front of one of the advertisements of the picture, reading it. He didn't see them.

"If you're thinking of going to see it, don't," Greda called to him. "It isn't worth the money."

He turned in surprise, then gave them a smile.

"What are you two girls doing out all alone?" he asked as he joined them.

"No one was kind enough to ask us for a date," Greda informed him.

Paul cast a glance at Lisa who remained silent.

"Would you join me for some refreshment?" he asked.

"We'd consider it," Greda told him. "Won't we, Lisa?"

"We might," Lisa said as she gave Paul a smile.

The three of them went to a café nearby and gave their order. They sat there for a while chatting and laughing. Lisa noticed that Paul seemed more like his old self. She wondered if it was because she hadn't been out with Hans. They took Greda home then walked on toward Lisa's home.

"Greda always seems so cheerful and so full of fun," Paul remarked. "I like her a lot. Don't you?"

Lisa agreed enthusiastically that she did. She smiled to herself as she thought that not too long ago she wouldn't have been so enthusiastic in her praise of Greda.

"Where's Hans?" Paul asked. "He's usually your shadow."

"Sometimes shadows just fade away," she told him. "Sometimes they're driven away by the sun when it shines."

"What does that remark mean?" he asked.

"You can take it for what it's worth," she replied.

"Does it mean that if I come around, I won't find him hanging around?"

"Suppose you come around and see," she suggested.

"I might do that," he told her.

He gave her hand a little squeeze as he told her good-night and it set her heart to pounding joyfully as he disappeared in the darkness.

CHAPTER 5

LISA HOPED THAT PAUL would come over the next evening and she waited eagerly for him. She put on a new
dress that her mother had just finished. She hoped that
Paul would like it. He didn't come and she was disappointed and then she became angry. She waited until it was
too late to hope that he would come, then she went out and
sat under her favorite tree while the dreams that were
never far from her thoughts drifted before her in succession
of bright pictures.

Paul was always the central figure in these dreams and
he was there tonight, even though she was angry with him
because he hadn't come. There was the dream of her wedding, when she and Paul would go to the next town to the
rabbi who would unite them in the ceremony of their forefathers. Paul would wear the small black cap which all
orthodox Jews still wore. She would wear the veil that her
mother had worn and her dress of white satin.

They would sip the wine and Paul would crush the
glass beneath his heel. They would receive the blessing
from the rabbi, then from their parents. She and Paul
would ride to their temporary home with her parents in the
car rented for the occasion. Perhaps not too long after
that they would be on their way to America. She would hate
to leave her parents and her friends, but her parents would
soon be following and they would be together in the land
of golden opportunities.

It made her happy to dream, even though she had no
assurance that the dream would ever become reality. Per-

haps Paul wouldn't want to leave his parents and go to America. Perhaps he was satisfied to remain here, even though the future was uncertain and fraught with danger. Perhaps he would never even ask her to marry him. Perhaps she had taken too much for granted. Her heart sank and the joy of her dreams left her.

She rose and went into the house. She saw the light in Paul's room as she stood by the window and she knew that at least he wasn't out with some other girl. That gave her some comfort, but she was depressed as she got into bed.

The next evening she didn't even look for him to come. After she had finished with the dishes, she went into the living room where her father was reading and got out a book. Presently Paul came. She recognized his step as he came up the walk and her heart kept time with his steps. He rang the bell and her mother went to answer. She heard her greeting Paul cordially and she heard him ask for her, but she didn't stir until her mother called to her that Paul was there.

She greeted him coolly. At his suggestion they went out to their favorite spot under the tree.

"I had planned to come over yesterday," he explained, "but I had to work late and by the time I got home and got cleaned up, I knew it would be too late to come over."

Her heart was suddenly light again and she felt like singing, but she greeted his remark with silence.

"It's been a long time since I've had a chance to talk to you alone," he continued as she remained silent. "Whenever I could come over, Hans was always here. Sometimes I felt like choking him. He acted as if you belonged to him. I thought that perhaps you did."

"I don't belong to anyone," she informed him.

"I always felt in my heart that you belonged to me," he said in tender tones. "I grew up with that thought and it wasn't until Hans became so attentive that I was afraid I had been mistaken. I was afraid that you loved him. That's not true, is it?" he asked anxiously.

"No, it isn't," she told him, thrilled by the tone of his

voice. "I never could love Hans for many reasons. But he was nice to me and we did have fun together. He took me places which I enjoyed, while you acted as if you didn't even want to be friends any longer."

"I didn't want to interfere, if you loved him," he explained. "If you could be happy with him, then that's what I wanted for you. I love you so much, Lisa, that your happiness means more to me than anything, even if it means giving you up to someone else."

He drew her to him and she didn't resist.

"I've waited a long time to tell you how much I love you," he said. "You're the center of my life, Lisa. Can you say that you care?"

He held her to him while he looked deep into her eyes and waited for her answer.

"I do care," she said in tones that were throbbing with joy. "It seems that I've loved you as long as I can remember, but you never told me and I was afraid that you didn't care."

He took her in his arms again and kissed her.

"We're both a couple of cowards, afraid of shadows," he said with a low laugh of sheer joy. "Now I can sleep at night instead of tossing and trying to forget the pain in my heart. Will you marry me, darling?"

"That's a silly question," she told him as she caressed his cheek. "I've been waiting to hear you ask that question. If I can't marry you, I'll never marry anyone because I'll never love anyone but you."

"I wish we could be married right away, but I don't want you to have to live on what I'm making now. I want you to have everything that you've been used to all your life. I'm expecting a better job soon and then I'll be making enough so that we can be married."

"I'll be happy with you, Paul, no matter how little we have."

"Suppose we wait until the Passover to tell our parents," he suggested. "I'm sure that by then I'll have that job and we can make plans for our wedding."

She agreed and they began to talk of the future. She

told him about her dream of going to America and she was even more happy when he told her that this was what he wanted also, though there seemed small chance of ever having it happen.

"We'll save every penny we can and we'll make the dream come true," she insisted. "We're both young and a few years will not seem too long. They say the steerage passage is cheap. Once we get to America, we'll soon find work, for I'll go to work, too, until we can get a little home where we can be happy."

"I wish we could go now instead of years from now," he said seriously. "There is talk that Hitler will soon be increasing his army. If that's true, then I'll have to go. If I go, I may never come back, or if I do, I may be too crippled to think of getting married."

"Don't say that!" she cried, putting her hand over his mouth. "Not tonight. Let's be happy in our dreams. Don't let such a nightmare blot them out. No matter how crippled you might be, I'd want to marry you anyway. If you never came back, I wouldn't want to live. But tonight let's just think of how happy we shall be together. I've dreamed of this night for a long time, Paul dear. Now that the dream has come true, I'm so happy that I can scarcely believe that I'm not still dreaming."

They talked of their plans until it was time for him to leave. She walked with him to the gate with his arm around her.

"I'm afraid Hans won't like it when he hears the news," Paul remarked. "He never did like me anyway. I saw him today and he glared at me and wouldn't even speak to me when I called to him across the street. I'm glad you don't love him. He would make any woman miserable, if she married him."

"Let's not think about Hans," she said. "What does it matter if he doesn't like you? I love you and that's all that matters to me."

Nevertheless Paul's remark remained with her as she

went into the house. She remembered what Hans had said and what her father had said about him. She remembered Hans' hinted threat and her fear returned. She tried to forget it, but the image of Hans pervaded her dreams like some grim ghost seeking vengeance and haunting her through the night.

CHAPTER 6

WHEN THE MORNING CAME, Lisa forgot the disturbing dreams and fears of the night. She remembered only the time spent under the tree when she had been in Paul's arms, when her lips had responded to his kiss and when she knew at last that this one dream had come true.

She was gay and sparkling at the table and her parents guessed the reason, that Paul had come back and everything was as it should be.

"I'm glad that Paul has come back," her mother remarked when she saw that Lisa did not intend to talk about what had happened.

"So am I," she replied. She was bursting with the desire to tell them the news. "And I'm glad that Hans doesn't come around any more."

"Your father and I were worried about Hans."

"You shouldn't have worried," Lisa told her. "I could never love Hans."

"We've always hoped that Paul would be the one, as you already know. He's a fine young man and I'm sure that he could make you happy."

"Mama! You're not trying to choose my husband for me, are you?" she asked with a provocative smile. "Do give me the privilege of choosing my husband. Parents just don't do that any more."

"No, but we can still hope, can't we?" Her mother gave her a tender smile.

"Sure you can. Just keep on hoping and perhaps everything will turn out the way you want it to. I'll try to be a dutiful daughter and choose the man you'd want me to marry. That is, if he'll have me. And after I've had time to look around."

She laughed a gay little laugh as they rose from the table and she helped her mother clear off the dishes while Nathaniel left for town.

All through the day Lisa sang little snatches of songs as she went about her work. Paul loved her, her heart kept singing. And he had dreams of America also. One day they would be there with a family around them and only happiness in their hearts. No more shadow of Hitler and his ambitious schemes for world power, no more fear of possible persecution. Only freedom from fear, from want and from foes within who might pose as friends.

No thought of Hans intruded upon the sheer joy of the present and dreams of the future. When evening came and the house had been put in order for the evening, she went out to sit under the tree. She waited impatiently for Paul, for it seemed ages since she had seen him. Funny how the world had changed overnight, she mused as she sat there. Strange how his coming meant more than it had ever meant before. She had never waited, tingling in every nerve, for the sound of his footsteps as he came down the walk, before last night. She had enjoyed having him near, but that had been all. Now her whole world seemed waiting breathless for his coming.

She heard the gate open and she waited eagerly for his approach. He came as she knew he would, without going to the door and asking for her and she rose to meet him. He took her in his arms and their lips met in a lingering caress.

"I thought the day would never end and I was so afraid that I would have to work tonight," he said.

"I wanted to tell Mama and Papa about us, but we agreed to wait so I'll wait, but it will be hard. The words almost popped out of my mouth this morning when they saw how happy I was."

"Let them worry a little while longer. My mother has been so worried that she's made life miserable for me.

She's been so afraid that you'd marry Hans. She wants you and no one else for a daughter-in-law."

"Then everyone will be happy, for that's just the way Mama and Papa have felt about you. I hope it won't be too long before I can belong to you." Then she added, "Whenever I think that perhaps war may come and take you away from me, I feel cold and sick all over. I couldn't stand it if that should happen."

He held her close. "Don't think such thoughts," he advised. "I'm sure it won't be long. Just today I learned that the job I was hoping for will be open for me in a few weeks. That means that we can be married this fall."

"Oh, dear! That seems forever. I wish we could be married now and wait for that new job together. I'd at least have you for a little while, no matter what happens."

"You have me, now and forever," he said as he kissed her.

As the days passed and Hans didn't return, Lisa thought that she was rid of him. She thought that his threats must have been only the bitter remarks of a boy who had been denied, for the first time, what he wanted and tried to obtain.

Finally, as the season of the Passover approached, Lisa and her mother were busy cleaning the house, even behind every piece of furniture and ornament, to be sure that there was no tiny speck of leaven in the house since during this time of celebration they ate unleavened bread.

When the time arrived for the Passover supper, Paul and Lisa's families met together. The eldest son of the family offered the prayer in the ritual before they partook of the meal of unleavened bread, chicken which had been killed and drained of blood, according to the law, and the herbs prescribed by their ancient law. Since there was no son in Nathaniel's family, Paul offered the prayer and pronounced the benediction before they ate. Nathaniel had always envied his friend for having this fine son while he had none, but he had hope that one day Paul would really be his son when he married Lisa.

When the meal was finished and the ceremonial solemnity was over, Paul cast a significant glance at Lisa and she gave him a smile of assent.

"I have something of importance to tell you," he announced.

There was silence while everyone waited for what he had to say.

"Lisa and I want to be married. Do I have your permission for us to become engaged?" he asked, turning to Nathaniel with a smile.

"Nothing could please me more than to say you have my permission," Nathaniel answered with a smile. "I've been hoping for this ever since you two were children."

"Thanks for saying yes, Papa," Lisa said, putting her arm around him as he sat near. "I would hate to displease you, but we would be married, even if you said no. I told you I'd have to choose my husband myself. But I think you knew all along that it would be Paul."

"I was hoping anyway," he said as he gave her a hug.

They spent the rest of the evening talking over plans for the wedding. Paul told them about his hoped-for new job and how this would enable them to be married in the fall.

"Lisa and I hope to go to America as soon as we can afford it," Paul told them. "When we get settled over there, then we can prepare for the rest of you to come over and join us."

"I wish we could all leave tomorrow," Nathaniel said, sighing deeply.

A shadow fell across the group and for a moment there was silence.

"What brought the sudden gloom, Nathaniel?" Herr Ermann asked. "Have you heard some bad news?"

"I heard that Hitler is increasing his army and he will lower the draft age," he replied. "That will include almost every young man in town."

Their conversation about the wedding and future plans came to an end. What had begun as such a joyful occasion ended in anxiety and gloom. Soon after, Herr Ermann and his wife left.

Paul lingered a while with Lisa. She clung to him in desperate fear.

"What if this should be true?" she cried. "If you have to go to war, I shall want to marry you, Paul, no matter what our plans might be for the future. I want to belong to you, no matter what happens. If you should get killed, I would want to die, too."

"Don't let such terrible thoughts mar the joy of today," he urged. "That may not happen. Hitler may be only bluffing. He can't fight the whole world and he may come to his senses before he tries. There isn't any war yet and there may never be one. Let's be happy in the present. I'm the happiest man in the world tonight, my darling. All I want is you, but I want your happiness above everything else, even my own life."

"Without your life there wouldn't be anything left in life for me," she said as she still clung to him.

"We'll live and be happy together, see if we don't," he whispered as he stroked her hair. "We'll live out our lives together, I'm sure."

"I shall try to pray that we may, but sometimes I wonder if there is a God or if He ever hears our prayers."

"Don't say such things," he rebuked her. "Just keep on praying and try to believe."

She tried to when she was alone in her room beside her bed, but the way to God seemed blocked by her own doubts. How could she believe when God didn't seem to care what happened to the people who called themselves the chosen of God? If they were, then why didn't God do something about them?

There was no answer and in her heart there was little faith. She crept into bed with a heavy heart and no assurance that there was a God who heard and answered prayer.

CHAPTER 7

Lisa's joy over her engagement was reflected in the hearts of her parents. Nathaniel's face beamed as he kissed her and his wife and left for town. He could scarcely wait to get there so that he could broadcast the news. Many of the ones he told knew Paul and they congratulated him on the prospects of having such a fine son-in-law.

Lisa's mother went about her work with a lighter heart than she had had for some time. The shadow of Hans had been removed and the future looked bright indeed. Nathaniel would have the son he had wanted all these years and perhaps there would be grandsons to carry on his name. She sang as she worked and Lisa glowed with the knowledge that her happiness had made them happy. All thoughts of possible war were for the time being forgotten.

"We must get to work on your trousseau," Elizabeth remarked when they had finished their morning tasks. "I shall have to get out my wedding dress and see if it is good enough for you to wear. I want you to have the best that we can afford. There must be nothing lacking in this wedding to make you completely happy. It is your great moment, my child, the one great day that will remain in your memory all the rest of your life."

"I'll be happy just to have Paul for my husband," Lisa said, while her eyes glowed with a happy light. "I shall want to wear your wedding dress, even if it's falling apart. Nothing could be more beautiful to me."

They went into the spare room and opened the big chest that stood by the window. Inside, carefully folded

43

and wrapped in a sheet was the wedding dress and the lace veil. The satin had aged until it was a pale ivory, but Lisa declared that it was even more beautiful than it must have been when it was new.

She held the veil up carefully and lowered it over her dark curls. It fell in a filmy cascade down her back.

"It will be just perfect," she murmured as she surveyed herself in the mirror. "I shall love wearing it, for I shall remember how happy you must have been wearing it yourself."

Her mother looked at her tenderly. "You will look like I did when I wore it," she remarked. "Seeing you in it, I will see myself as I was then. I had no idea how much you look like I did when I was your age."

Lisa threw her arms around her mother and whispered, "I wouldn't want to look like anyone else. I'm glad I look like you. You're beautiful, more beautiful than I'll ever be."

Her eyes turned to the dresser where her mother's picture stood in her wedding gown.

They took out the dress and examined it carefully. When they saw that there was nothing to mar its loveliness, they put the things carefully back in the chest.

"You two can live cheaply with us," Elizabeth remarked, "so you'll soon save enough for your trip to America. I'll hate to see you go, but when you go, your father will feel justified in getting rid of his business so that we can join you. He's been afraid to venture before now. It takes youth to strike out into unknown paths."

"It seems such a long time until fall," Lisa sighed.

"The time will pass quickly. There is much to be done. I'll get started right away with the sewing. It will be such fun," she said with a bright smile.

They went to town that afternoon and began their shopping. Paul came that evening and they spent an hour or two under the tree talking of the future. Lisa felt that

these defenseless neighboring countries by the mere use of force. He had increased his army rapidly with young men from every quarter. His Gestapo were active in confiscating property so that his treasury could amply meet his increasing needs.

England prepared for war with frantic haste while Hitler massed his armies at the border, preparing to invade Sudetenland. In October the land was invaded and Czechoslovakia, left alone to defend itself after refusing to yield at the suggestion of appeasement, was invaded and taken over by the hordes under the madman of Berlin.

When news of the impending war drifted into the town, fear filled every heart, but terror overwhelmed the Jewish families. They knew only too well what they might expect. Most of the young men of military age were ordered to report for duty. Hans was one of those who went with the first contingent. Before he left, he came to see Paul.

"I'll be leaving tomorrow for the army," he said.

He hadn't seen Paul since Paul had returned home. He had gone to the hospital only once after that first bitter meeting. Paul had tried to be civil, but there had been few words between them.

"I just want you to know," he said, "that I'm keeping my promise to see that you have all that you need until you're able to return to work. I've deposited money in the bank in your account and if that isn't enough, my father will take care of the rest. That is, if I don't return. If I don't, I suppose you wouldn't shed any tears."

Paul looked at him gravely and said, "I'm only sorry that I have to take anything from you."

"You took away from me what I wanted most in life, so you shouldn't mind taking my money. That doesn't count," Hans retorted.

Paul watched him go and he tried to conquer the hatred that rose within him at the sight of him and the memory of that car which was heading toward him when he was trying frantically to get out of its way.

When Lisa came over a little while after Hans had left,

Paul told her what he had said about the money. He didn't tell her that last remark of Hans. Lisa felt almost glad that Paul had had the accident. At least he wouldn't have to join the army. Even if he did have to limp the rest of his life, he would be alive and if he had to go to war, much worse might happen to him.

"I'm glad that you don't have to go," she said. "How terrible it would be if you went and came home blind or crippled."

She realized that she had said the wrong thing when she saw the look he gave her.

"That's been taken care of already by our friend Hans," he said bitterly.

From the beginning of hostilities Hitler had singled out the Jews as his special target. His demon-inspired hatred of them urged him to use every means of torture that his twisted brain could devise. Their lands were seized, their property was confiscated and they were driven like cattle to prison camps where many met a merciful death from exposure and starvation before they were put to torture.

When the news spread that Hitler seemed determined to exterminate the Jews, as the fires of war spread and the whole world seemed destined to be involved, hundreds tried to leave the country. They swarmed over the borders in the frantic effort to escape the merciless troops which sought them. The border countries closed their doors to further refugees. They were afraid of reprisals from Hitler's soldiers. Their refusal didn't save them, for they were hurled into the maelstrom and crushed by the invading armies which seemed destined to make possible Hitler's dream of world conquest.

When news of the atrocities being perpetrated against the helpless Jews reached the town where Paul and Lisa lived, they all prepared to flee, but they learned before they fled that it was too late. There was no escape, except the dangerous attempt to slip singly through the lines and across the border to France. Perhaps, if they reached France, they might be able to reach England. It was indeed dangerous and hopeless from the beginning, but a few tried it. They were shot as they neared the border. The news drifted in and added terror to those remaining. They could only wait for the worst. There was no hope of escape.

All thought of Lisa's wedding was forgotten. Nothing remained of all the bright dreams. There was nothing left but the daily anxiety and fear of what might come to them.

The war dragged on, but for some reason the little town was not molested. While other towns were being bombed and wrecked, this one escaped. It was not in the line of attack by either force and had no strategic importance.

As anxiety dogged the days and nights of the Jewish residents, Paul was finally able to put his crutches aside. His strength had almost returned and the doctor had proved correct in his diagnosis, that one leg would be as good as new. The other, however, was still lame and he walked with a bad limp. He knew that it would always be that way and he realized that the doctor had mercifully withheld the truth from him. He learned to accept it without bitterness and tried to make the best of it. He and Lisa never spoke of the wedding, for the time had long since passed.

When that day had arrived they were making frantic preparations to flee, and since then they had accepted the fact that as long as the war lasted and their own fate hung so dangerously in the balance, they could not think of marriage. Lisa would have been willing to have a quiet wedding, for, just as she had told Paul, it would bring her joy if she could only belong to him for a little while, no matter what the future might hold. But even if Paul had been willing, there was no rabbi to perform the ceremony. The one who was in the next town had fallen a victim to Hitler's destruction. They would have been afraid to apply for a license to be married by the town justice, for they were trying to escape notice from everyone, although their neighbors were still kind and friendly. Fear had not yet made them enemies.

As time passed, their fears subsided somewhat. They

hoped that Hitler would be too much engrossed with the
war which he now seemed to be losing, to vent his hatred
upon them. When the news of the success of the allies began to seep in, they took heart and hope began to live within
them. Then, almost at the end, just before the Normandy
invasion, the Gestapo entered the town and tragedy reached
its climax.

They began their work of destruction in the business
section of the town. Herr Bergen's shop was looted and the
contents loaded on trucks, then the place was set on fire.
The few other business places of the Jews were treated
likewise. They seemed to have the list of every Jewish
establishment and the addresses of every Jew in town.
When they had finished their work in the business section,
they proceeded to the homes.

Lisa was sitting in Paul's home with him when she
saw them coming.

"The soldiers!" she cried. "They're coming for us!"

Paul took her in his arms and she clung to him.

"Just remember, darling," he said, "if we're separated,
that I love you with my whole soul, more than life itself.
If we're allowed to live, come back here. No matter how
long it may be, I'll be here waiting for you. I'll get back
somehow, if I'm alive. Come back, Lisa, for I'll come back
and wait for you."

"Oh, Paul!" she cried. "Don't let them take you away
from me! O God, don't let us be separated!"

There was no time for more words, for the soldiers
had arrived. Paul was seized and taken to join the others
walking behind the soldiers, herded together like animals.
Another soldier led Lisa away to another group on the
other side of the street.

"Please let me go with him!" she begged the soldier
who held her.

He told her to shut up and struck her across her mouth,
cutting her lip.

She heard one of the soldiers call to another, "This
one is crippled. He won't get far on that game leg."

"Be glad. One less to worry with. It would be easier if we could kill them all here. Then we wouldn't have to bother taking them so far."

"We've got better things waiting for them," another remarked, laughing harshly.

Lisa was petrified with fright, but her one thought was to get a last look at Paul. It might well be her last look and her terror turned to the numbness of despair. At last the thing had come which they had feared all these months, and now hope was gone forever.

She saw her mother in the group waiting for their arrival. She managed to whisper and ask about her father, while they waited for the order to march.

"They clubbed him to death when he protested at the looting of his store," her mother told her brokenly. "I was there and saw it all. I was just going to the store. They took me after I watched him die. I couldn't even go to him."

Like her mother, Lisa was so numb that she couldn't shed a tear. She seemed bereft of the ability to suffer. She could feel no emotion but despair. She looked at her mother and she saw that Elizabeth seemed suddenly to have become an old woman. Her eyes were sunken as if she were already dead, with black circles beneath them and pallid lips that had once been so lovely. She knew that her mother was already dead within. Nothing that those demons in Berlin would do to her could matter now. She feared that it would not be long before her mother would die physically, for her heart was broken.

Lisa's own heart turned to stone. Where was the Lord God of Elijah? Where was the God who had promised them that they should one day be chief among the nations in the land where David had been king? Where was that God and why was He allowing them to be punished in this terrible way? Why did He say that He loved Israel with an everlasting love? Was this love? Surely there wasn't any God. If there was, He had forgotten His people. He hadn't kept His word. No need to pray. All their prayers had been wasted. She'd never pray again. What was the use? God no longer cared what happened to them, if He was still in existence.

One of the soldiers gave an order and they turned their horses around and rode out of town. Behind them walked the people marked for torture and death, the people whom God had seemed to forget.

CHAPTER 10

THE WEARY, TERRIFIED PRISONERS marched for miles and
endless hours, it seemed, until they reached a railroad
and were jammed in freight cars with other prisoners.
They rode through the night and into the next day without
food or water. Other prison camps had been emptied by the
various means that Hitler and his aides in beastliness had
devised. Many prisoners had dug their own graves, then
had been shot and covered up in the long trenches, many
of them still alive. Others had been burned to death and
had met death by other cruel means. The camp to which
Lisa and her mother were taken was far from Berlin and
nearer the French border. These new prisoners were the
gleanings that been overlooked when the mass slaughters
had taken place. Just now Hitler was fighting for survival
in the last struggle which would bring about his final defeat.

The group to which Paul had been assigned was headed
in another direction. Their march was longer and more
prostrating. Some fell by the way. They were beaten until
they struggled to their feet or else clubbed to death and
left while the others struggled on.

Paul managed to keep on his feet for a time, though he
fell behind the others. He struggled to keep going, for he
was hoping that by some miracle he would be saved as well
as Lisa. He had heard rumors of the crisis of the war. His
one hope was that the war would end before they were
slaughtered.

Every step caused pain, for he had not yet regained
even a partial use of the badly injured leg, but he hobbled
doggedly on, though he felt his strength ebbing out and he

was afraid that if they couldn't reach the end of their march soon, he'd also fall on the road and that would be the end.

He had heard one of the troopers say that the railroad shouldn't be much farther away. He struggled to keep on his feet, but he felt himself weakening and the pain was almost unbearable. The world began to spin around and he struggled to keep his footing. They refused to support him and he dropped to the ground where he lay moaning and struggling frantically to rise. Then everything was blotted out as he lost consciousness.

One of the troopers saw him fall and rode back to where he lay.

"Get up, you swine, if you don't want a beating," he said. "We don't have much farther to go."

When Paul didn't answer he turned his body over with his boot. When he saw the closed eyes and the lifeless body, he called to the others, "I think this crippled one's dead. What shall I do about him?"

"Club him and leave him," the officer ordered. "One less to bother with. He should be glad he died before worse happened to him."

The trooper hit Paul with the butt of his gun, then left him. Night came and the air was chill. Paul finally opened his eyes and tried to recall where he was and what had happened. The blow upon his head had stunned him. He tried to rise, but he fell back, weak and dizzy. He lay there for a while, while he recalled what had happened. Horror swept over him as he remembered his last sight of Lisa as she went with the others down the road away from him. He knew he would never forget that sight, the droop of her shoulders, the lovely head bowed in utter despair, the hopeless attitude of the others.

He saw Lisa turn for a last look at him but he couldn't be sure that she had seen him. Her face was white, as if it had been carved from marble, and he could see that the light had died from her eyes. She looked as if she had already seen death and was only waiting for it to strike. The memory of that scene pierced through his mind and into his

heart and agony held him in its grip. He tried once more
to get on his feet and this time he succeeded.

He turned back toward his home. He knew that it
would be desolate and filled only with painful memories,
for his mother and father had been taken away also, but
it was his only haven of refuge. If the soldiers thought
that he was dead, he might have a chance to hide, if he
could just get back home. He must live, if only to wait and
hope that Lisa would also escape death.

As he struggled on, walking slowly and resting at intervals, he prayed as he had never prayed before. Though
he had never had the bitterness toward God that Lisa had
in her heart, still God seemed far away and he had to admit
when he and Lisa had argued about it, that God didn't
seem interested in His people any longer. But now in this
desperate hour when there was no one else to turn to, he
turned to the God of his people.

"God, help me to get back home," he cried over and
over. "If You still care for any of us, help me and help
Lisa. Don't let them kill her! End this war and save the
rest of us."

He seemed to feel renewed strength, though he didn't
even wonder if it was an answer to prayer, but he continued to struggle on in spite of the pain. Hope grew within
him as he began to see familiar landmarks and he knew
that he was not far from home.

Just as the first faint streak of light began to split the
darkness, he saw the outlines of the houses and he struggled to walk faster, even though the pain was agonizing
and though he fell often. He wondered, as he struggled on,
if this night's ordeal had injured his leg further. Even that
possibility didn't matter now. Nothing mattered but the
hope of getting home and of being able to find out what
had happened to Lisa.

He was glad that it was too early for anyone to be
stirring. He wanted to get inside his house before daylight
came. As he reached the street where his home stood, he
stopped and stared in horror at the spot where his home

had been. It was a heap of charred ruins. Across the street, charred wood and crumbling brick told the same sad story. Both houses had been burned by the ruthless destroyers.

He stood staring at the ruins and wondering where he could go and what he could do. He had had no plans after he reached home, but it had been his one hope of refuge. Now there was nothing and he didn't know how he could exist with no place to live, nowhere to hide.

While he stood there exhausted and deep in despair, he saw a door open and someone came out of the house where he stood against the gate. He uttered a sharp cry as he recognized Greda. The sight of Greda brought everything back and the pain seemed more than he could bear. He didn't even wonder why she should be up at this early hour. He only knew that she was there, a friend whom he had never hoped to see again.

Greda heard the faint cry and turned startled eyes toward him. When she recognized the huddled figure leaning against the fence, she hurried to him.

"Paul!" she cried and began to sob. "I thought I'd never see you again. Oh, I'm so glad that you're still alive! Come on inside and tell me what happened."

She helped him as he leaned upon her for support. Now that he had reached the end of his journey, his strength suddenly left him and he felt faint and sick. She took him into the living room and let him lie on the couch.

"I'll get some hot milk for you in a jiffy," she said and went into the kitchen.

She returned shortly and held it for him while he sipped it slowly. He hadn't realized that he was hungry and the milk revived him. When he had finished, he lay back again with a sigh.

"How wonderful to lie on a soft cushion," he sighed. "How wonderful to find you and to have you for a friend. And such a wonderful friend! I didn't realize that I was in front of your house until you came out and I recognized you. An angel couldn't have looked more beautiful."

"That's the first time I've ever been called beautiful,"

she said with the same gay smile that he had seen so often before. It warmed his heart and eased his pain just a little.

"I've been crying ever since they took you away," Greda told him. "I tried to sleep, but I couldn't and I finally got up and went outside. I thought I'd go over and see if there was anything left in the two ruins that I might be able to save for you if you ever came back. How glad I am that I came out just when I did. Tell me what happened to make them let you go."

"They didn't let me go. They left me for dead," he said, then he told her what had happened.

"I don't suppose you could know where they took Lisa," he said.

"No, no one knows anything about where any of them went. The whole town was horrified. We all felt as if our own loved ones had just died."

"I must try to find Lisa," Paul said. "I'll never have another peaceful minute until I know where she is, or what they did to her."

"You can't do anything but wait and hope," she told him. "If they know that you're still alive, you'll only be taken again and killed. Let's hope that the war will end before they have a chance to harm any of the ones who were taken from here."

"You're right," he sighed. "But I'll always feel guilty if I'm alive and she is dead."

"We'll pray that she will live and that one day you two will be happy together," she said gently as she stroked his head.

"You'll have to pray for both of us," he said. "I prayed back there on the road, but I'm afraid I don't have much faith in prayer."

"I never mentioned this before, Paul, for I know that you don't believe in Jesus Christ. But I believe that He is the Son of God. I've been taught to pray in His name and that God will answer prayer if we pray in the name of His Son. I don't know much about religion, but I do believe that, so I'll pray for you and Lisa."

"Thanks," he murmured. "You're a wonderful friend. It's good to rest here for a little while, but I'll have to find some place to stay until the danger has passed. Now that I don't have a home any longer, I don't know just what to do. I'll have to think it over."

"You'll stay right here with us," she said. "I know that Mama and Papa will be glad to let you stay here until the war is over. We can keep you hidden, so that if they come this way again, they won't find you. I don't think they will come again, for they've cleaned out the town and they think you're dead, so you'll be safe, unless some Nazi spy should see you. We won't let that happen."

"I don't want to bring any danger to you," he objected.

"Let us worry about that," she said. "Now you rest here while I go and get breakfast started. I'll waken Papa and Mama and tell them the good news."

Presently they came in and greeted Paul cordially, telling him how glad they were that he had escaped. They insisted that he stay with them until they saw how the war would end. Until the war ended, he would be safe with them.

He tried to tell them how grateful he was, but even while he was talking, he fell asleep from sheer exhaustion. They slipped out and left him sleeping.

Greda came in later and stood looking down at him while the tears trickled down her cheeks. He looked so pathetic, with his hair rumpled and his face streaked with dirt. The deep circles under his eyes told her how he had suffered physically, but she knew that the physical pain was nothing to the agony in his heart.

"Oh, Paul darling," she said to herself, "if you only knew how I suffer for you and for myself. I want you to have Lisa, for I know how much you love her and that she alone can make you happy, but you'll never know how much I love you and how I suffer when I know that I can never have your love, because it belongs to her."

She stooped down and brushed his forehead gently with her lips, while a tear dropped upon his rumpled hair, then she left him and went to join her mother in the kitchen.

CHAPTER 11

DURING THE LONG MARCH to the train Lisa walked in silence. She was glad that she was beside her mother, so that at least they could share their sorrow. There was nothing that could take away the suffering at the memory of the terrible tragedy that had just occurred.

Elizabeth walked like one in a dream. She seemed dazed and stricken so deeply that she appeared to have no awareness of her surroundings. She stared before her with eyes that saw nothing. She was looking in memory upon that scene when she had stood helpless while the husband she adored was clubbed to death.

Lisa spoke to her once or twice, but, if she heard, she didn't answer. The girl's heart ached for her own sorrow, but still more for the suffering she knew her mother was enduring. She couldn't even give her a caress. She longed to take her mother in her arms and talk to her until the wall of shock was broken down and the tears could flow. She couldn't even cry over her own sorrow. The shock had left her numb and shaken, but she had hope, though only a faint hope, that Paul was still alive, while her mother had none.

She became exhausted and she wondered how much longer she could hold out. One of the group had dropped to the road exhausted and she had been shot and left there dying. It made Lisa wonder about Paul and brought her fears back with renewed horror. She knew that he would never be able to make a long march with his injured leg. What if he had fallen behind and had already been shot?

The thought brought torture and she almost cried aloud. She put her hand over her mouth to keep back that cry. She must be brave for her mother's sake. Perhaps when they reached their destination she would be able to talk to her and try to comfort her in her grief.

The prospect of what the end of the trip might be for all of them brought fear that mingled with her grief. She knew they had little hope that they would escape death and she wondered what mode of torture their captors had devised. She hoped that if they were destined for torture, she and her mother would both die a merciful death before then. Hope of ever seeing Paul again faded as they came at last to the station and waited for the freight cars which were to take them to their destination.

She was amazed at her mother's strength, for she did not seem to tire as she walked doggedly along, oblivious of everything. She wasn't exhausted like many of the others who fell upon the ground and lay there when they finally stopped and waited for the train to arrive. All of those others had dragged weary feet to the end of their march, for they had seen what would happen to them if they fell by the wayside. Though they realized that death by this means would perhaps be more merciful than the torture which others of their race had endured, still there remained a glimmer of hope.

For Elizabeth there was no hope. Her spirit was already dead and as Lisa looked at her with pain-filled eyes, she felt that her mother would not survive her father very long.

When at last they reached their destination in the filthy camp where they would exist until the war ended or until they were slaughtered, most of the women and girls in the crude barracks where they were quartered fell across the bunks and dropped off to sleep, though they were hungry and thirsty. Elizabeth sat on the side of her bunk and stared before her with eyes that seemed to see nothing. Lisa tried to persuade her to lie down, telling her that she must get some rest or she would be sick.

For the first time since they had begun their march she seemed aware of Lisa's presence. She stared at her dully, then said in a hollow voice, "That would be the best thing that could happen to me. The sooner I die, the better off I'll be."

"Don't feel that way, Mama, dear," Lisa begged, taking her mother in her arms and holding her close. "Then I would be all alone. I need you, Mama. Papa would want you to stay with me. Don't go and leave me."

"We'll all be gone soon," she said in that same dead voice. "What does it matter if I go before you?"

Lisa used every power that she possessed to make her mother cry. She felt that the tears would be a release, but the tears wouldn't come. Finally she did consent to lie down and Lisa crept into the narrow bunk beside her and tried to sleep, but sleep wouldn't come. She lay there worn and weary, wondering what had happened to Paul, if he would ever live to return home, or if she had seen him for the last time. He had said he would be there waiting for her when the war was over. She wondered if she would ever live to return there, even if, by some miracle, he did. She felt that she never would. She hoped that if she had to die, death would come swiftly and that she would meet it bravely. She didn't even think of praying. God no longer existed in her thoughts.

When morning came someone came in with weak broth and black bread. That was to last them until evening. They were allowed to clean up their filthy quarters as best they could. There was little enthusiasm in the attempt when there was little bedding, nothing upon the bunks but hard mattresses that were filthy, no sheets, only a thin, dirty blanket. Their food was scarcely enough to keep them from starving, but what did it matter to those who guarded them if they starved? They were to die anyway and they might just as well die by starvation as by other means.

Lisa became thinner as the days passed. Dark circles

appeared under her eyes and they no longer shone with the light that had made them so beautiful. They were luster-less and her lips had lost their color. She existed through the endless days by sheer force of will. It would have been easier, far easier, to lie down and die and she longed to do that, but the hope that kept her alive was that perhaps — just perhaps — Paul was still alive and might one day be waiting for her.

As time passed and no word came for their immediate slaughter, she began to hope that, after all, they might be spared. This prison camp was farthest removed from the region where most of the fighting was taking place and as the crisis of the war approached, only the camps with the largest number of Jews came under Hitler's orders for their destruction. The others could wait until later, when he was more sure of victory. He already had what wealth they possessed, so he could take his time in his effort to destroy the whole race within his borders.

Lisa became more concerned about her mother as time passed. Elizabeth displayed no indication that she knew what was going on around her. She seldom spoke except to answer some question that Lisa put to her and even then, she often seemed not to understand. Lisa saw her fading slowly day by day, for she often refused to eat. Lisa felt that she was trying to die. Her heart was torn with added grief and dread for the day when she would be left alone, but she tried not to give way to her grief, for she didn't want her mother to see her crying.

One morning when she got up with the others, she climbed down from her bunk and leaned over her mother to kiss her and waken her. She thought she was still asleep until she touched the cold lips and saw that her mother was not breathing. She dropped beside the bed and gave way to the sobs that she had restrained for so long and wept wildly and uncontrolled. Those who had become her friends came over and tried to console her, but she waved them off while she continued to let her grief express itself in sobs.

Finally one of the prison workers came in and ordered her to get up so that they could take the body out and bury it. She begged him to let her go with him, but he ordered her roughly to stay where she was. Someone came in to help him and they dragged the still form out by the arms as if it had been the body of some animal, while Lisa turned her head away and wept. She knew how her mother would be buried. At the far end of the camp enclosure there was a trench. It was shallow and it was filled with others who had died from starvation and exposure. Lime would be thrown over the loved form and then a shovel or two of earth would be thrown over it so that the stench would not be too strong.

Lisa wished that she could die. Not even the hope of seeing Paul again made her want to live, but as the dreary days passed into weeks, the acuteness of suffering passed and only a dull ache remained.

From the beginning of the war, the underground band of patriots worked faithfully in their effort to free prisoners and to help refugees escape across the border. Many of them lost their lives, but others took their places. Toward the end of the war, when Hitler knew that he would stand or fall by the next move of the allies, some of those in the underground who had watched this camp for some time were determined that they would do what they could to release as many of the prisoners as possible before they were tortured. They had spent hours during the nights digging a tunnel that reached within the prison enclosure, near the spot where Lisa and the others were housed. One of them slipped through and in the darkness made his way to the shack. He waited for a shadowy form to come outside, and then whispered that a few of them could attempt to make their way to the tunnel and out to freedom. The prisoner was warned to tell only a few and to bind them to secrecy, for if all of them attempted to escape, there would be panic and certain capture, for the guards would discover them and they would be shot down in their attempt.

She told Lisa and a few others who bunked near her and they waited nervously for the appointed time to slip out of the shack. They went to bed as usual and pretended to sleep, but when the others seemed to be asleep, they left their bunks one by one and slipped out into the darkness.

To Lisa, what happened after that seemed more of a dream than reality. There was the long march through dense woods, at times crawling upon their stomachs to keep out of sight as they neared the border and the patrols were more numerous and alert. They felt intense relief when at last they could rest for a little while in the shelter of dense bushes, knowing that they were at last out of reach of the border patrol and Hitler's menace.

There was still danger for the little group, for Hitler's spies were still on the alert in France. They wouldn't be safe until they were on their way to England, and even then they might be bombed, for England was still enduring the raids which never ceased until the Normandy invasion finally began to succeed.

During the day they rested, with little to eat, weary and cold, but with hope rising within them. Lisa had no hope, just the inborn will to live. Instead of being able to go back to her home where she could wait for Paul while hope lasted that he was alive, she was on her way to an unknown future.

When night came they traveled, led by their faithful guides. They were met at intervals by some of the underground who supplied them with food and gave directions to their guides. At last they reached the coast after endless miles and endless walking until feet became sore and limbs ached with the effort to keep going.

There were two small boats waiting for them when they reached the coast across the channel from England. Fortunately the channel was calm and the captain of the craft hoped to make it safely across before any rough weather descended upon them.

In the early dawn of a gray, foggy morning, they

landed on the coast of the only country that held out a welcome hand to any refugees who might reach their shore. Though England was fighting for her very existence, she was willing to share what she had with others who had less.

They were met by those who had news of their arrival. It was remarkable how skillfully those in this movement of mercy found the means to communicate and how they managed to meet every emergency, even though they exposed themselves to death.

They were guided to a small hut not far from where they landed and were given hot broth and warm clothing and allowed to rest until evening. A few days later they were put on board a ship bound for America.

Lisa stood at the rail and looked at the shores of England receding in the fogged atmosphere of the night and there were conflicting emotions within her. She was bound for the land of which she had dreamed, for which she and Paul had planned in that happy past which seemed as if it never existed. There was danger that they might be torpedoed and never reach their destination and she almost wished that this would happen. Her dream would be realized if they landed safely, but the dream had become a nightmare. She would be arriving alone. No loving husband beside her, no plans for the parents to follow. There was no one but herself and she didn't want to face the future alone.

The land which had once seemed the land of opportunity, the land at the end of the rainbow, had suddenly become a wilderness where she would wander alone, with none to care.

She went below to her cabin where she wept silently. It would be easy to slip over the side of the boat and sink beneath the waves. There would be oblivion beneath the waves. There was no life beyond this one. She was convinced of that. If there was a God and a heaven, He would have saved His people for it, but He hadn't done it. Death was the end and that was that.

She half rose to go outside and climb over the rail,

but something held her back. It was the thought that per-haps Paul had also escaped and that someday he might be there at home waiting for her. Somehow she must get back to her home when this war was over and find out the truth. She could never spend another happy moment until she knew. That might take years, but if it took a lifetime, she would still go back and learn the truth.

CHAPTER 12

THE SUN WAS SHINING BRIGHTLY as the ship approached New York harbor. The refugees crowded on deck where they caught their first sight of the Statue of Liberty. Many of them had heard of it but never expected to see it, the lady with the torch of freedom held high to all who might come to her shores.

They were bewildered and broken, these helpless ones who had been delivered from the jaws of death and were being brought to this new land and an unknown future. Many were so burdened with grief over the loss of loved ones that there was no light of hope within them. The future held no promise of happiness. It would be mere existence with heart-breaking memories that they would carry through the years. There were others who had not known such grief, but who knew that they had barely escaped Hitler's tortures and when they saw the great statue in the morning sun, they let out a glad shout and began to wave their hands and utter exclamations of joy in their native tongue.

Lisa stood alone, apart from the others gathered in the bow of the ship. She had expected to be thrilled as these were at the sight of the statue, but that had been when she and Paul would see it together. Now there was nothing in her heart but deadness, no feeling that she could define. There wasn't even the desire to weep. She stared at it apathetically. Her one desire from now on would be to get back home. If Paul should be alive, then they might still find happiness. If he was dead, then it didn't matter what happened.

When the ship docked, the refugees were marched

from the ship to the immigration station where committees were waiting to care for them. It was a herculean task that these groups had taken upon themselves, to see that homes were provided for them and to find employment for those who might be qualified for some kind of work. The government was doing its utmost to take care of these helpless and destitute refugees, many of them having only the clothes they wore when they had escaped, but it still remained for large-hearted individuals to try to meet the needs of individuals under their care.

They were arranged into groups and each one interviewed. Some had relatives living in the States and their problem was comparatively easy. Transportation was arranged for them to go to the homes of these relatives. Others were sent to various shelters or homes that were opened to them by generous ones who were glad to help in this time of emergency.

When Lisa was interviewed, her knowledge of English was a help in getting her placed. When she was asked if she would be willing to work in some home as a maid, she said that she was willing to do anything that she felt capable of doing.

She was taken to an employment agency and soon she was on her way to a wealthy home in the suburbs. Her employer, Mrs. Gaynor, had offered to take someone if the person could speak English. She had fired one of her maids and thought that Lisa could fill her place.

The moment Lisa saw Mrs. Gaynor, she knew that she wouldn't like this woman. She was middle-aged, and attractive, but her eyes were cold and hard. She met Lisa without a smile and cast a disapproving look at her, then turned to the person at the agency.

"Is this the best that you could do?" she asked with a note of irritation. "She could at least have been cleaned up."

The lady in the office was indignant at her tone and she answered rather sharply.

"Madam, this girl has been in a prison camp for months

and she escaped by traveling miles through mud and cold. How could you expect her to look spic and span? She was fortunate to escape with her life. Our organization is doing all it can to help these people, but there are limitations. If you don't want her, we can find some other place for her."

Lisa was truly a pitiful sight. She had washed her hair and had bathed on ship board, but she couldn't do anything about her clothes. They were a sorry sight. They were torn and begrimed. She was haggard and hollow-eyed. Little trace of her beauty remained. She couldn't blame the lady for not wanting her.

"I'll keep my word," Mrs. Gaynor replied haughtily, feeling rebuked by the other's words. "I suppose I can get her cleaned up. You may come with me," she said to Lisa.

She followed her employer to her car and they drove to her home in silence. Lisa followed her into the house.

"I believe you speak English," Mrs. Gaynor said when they went inside. "That was one of the stipulations."

"Yes, I speak English," Lisa replied.

Mrs. Gaynor rang a bell and a maid appeared.

"Take this girl and see if she can wear any of the uniforms," she said. "But see that she gets a bath first. She doesn't look as if she's had one for ages. And throw away those dirty rags she's wearing."

Lisa's anger seethed within her and she felt like telling her employer that she wouldn't stay, but she managed to keep silent as she followed the maid upstairs.

When they were alone, the maid said, "That old dragon will surely put you through the mill. She pays well, or she wouldn't have any help, but she makes up for it by being the meanest woman alive. I would quit today if I could find another job that paid like this one."

"I think I shall hate her," Lisa said frankly.

"You will. We all do," was the other maid's encouraging remark.

The days that followed were days of trial for Lisa. She told herself that she had escaped from one prison to find herself in another. Though there was no fear of physical torture in this prison, she endured mental torture throughout every day. Nothing ever satisfied Mrs. Gaynor. Her commands seemed to be given to purposely hurt her and to make her feel her inferiority. If this was a sample of the land of opportunity, it was far from what she had pictured in her dreams.

She was not allowed to leave the house except on her one afternoon off. When Sunday came, Mrs. Gaynor and her husband dressed in their best and drove to church. Lisa watched them with a bitter gleam in her dark eyes. These people called themselves Christians. What hypocrites they were! She thought of the friends back home who professed to believe that Jesus of Nazareth was the Son of God and who worshiped Him in their own way. What a contrast those friends were from these two, for Mr. Gaynor was no better than his wife. Servants were little better than animals to them. They showed more kindness to the little dog which had the run of the house than they did to their servants.

If these two people were a fair sample of American Christians, she thought she would hate them all.

Weeks passed and Lisa wondered how she could get away from there and try to find another position. She felt helpless and she didn't know where the employment office was. Mrs. Gaynor hadn't noticed that her new maid was changing rapidly from the haggard, half-starved girl she had first seen, into the beauty she had once been. Even though Lisa still bore the scars on her heart and in her soul, she was well fed and her youth and vigor responded.

There was a party one evening at the Gaynor home and the maids were all on duty to serve. Lisa was stationed at the punch bowl which was liberally spiked with the finest liquor. She served the guests without incident during the early part of the party. She noticed a certain young man who came again and again to the table to be served. Finally the liquor began to have its effects. He had observed Lisa when he first came in and she felt that he was watching her with a look which she knew well, for she had seen it in the eyes of others back at home. She thought nothing of it, for she wasn't thinking about her looks. She hadn't even noticed that she had blossomed into restored beauty. She had once gloried in her beauty, but it had been for Paul, that she might appear beautiful in his eyes. Now there was no longer any need for beauty.

Finally the young man began to talk to her as he stood drinking.

"You're about the prettiest person here tonight," he remarked in a voice that was already thick from too much liquor.

Lisa didn't answer and he set his glass down and bent over her.

"Didn't you hear what I said?" he asked. "I like pretty girls and you're as pretty as any I've seen. How about a date after this dull party is over?"

"Please go away and leave me alone," Lisa said. She saw Mrs. Gaynor's eyes fastened upon them and she could see that the woman was furious.

"I won't go away without your promise to meet me outside after the party," he insisted.

He caught hold of her hand and she struggled to release it. As she did so, she upset the punch bowl. It fell off the silver stand where it rested and hit the floor with a crash and a splash of liquid on the carpet. The guests stared in amazement while Mrs. Gaynor bore down upon them blazing with fury.

"What does this mean?" she asked the young man, but she was looking at Lisa.

"I was only trying to make a date with your pretty maid," the young man explained with a laugh as he surveyed the wreckage. "I'll gladly pay for the damages. I'm sorry if I've broken up your party. Guess I had a little too much of this good punch. You shouldn't have made it so tempting."

She ignored him and turned upon Lisa.

"Go to your room and pack your things. And get out of here."

"See here, you can't turn her out into the night," the young man protested. "Where do you think she could go at this hour?"

"I'll give you until morning," she conceded. "I think you'd better leave, Mr. Young," she said, then turned to give an order to another maid to clean up the mess.

"Sorry I caused so much trouble," the young man told Lisa contritely.

"Don't be sorry," she told him as she turned away. "I'm glad I'm going. This place is almost as bad as a prison camp. I hate it."

The next morning, with her few possessions in a suitcase, she left the house. She didn't know where she would go or what she could do, but she was glad to get away. Mrs. Gaynor had told her the name of the employment agency and she had phoned for a taxi, so that the girl wouldn't get lost. She hated to see Lisa go, for she had been better than the other maids, but she refused to do what she thought would be beneath her dignity, to tell Lisa that she might stay.

Lisa had one small comfort. She had some money saved. Mrs. Gaynor had paid her well. She would put that aside and save it for the one purpose in her life, to get back home and look for Paul.

When she entered the agency, the lady in the office said that she had no opening for her. She told Lisa to come back in a day or so and that perhaps by then there might be something.

"But I have no place to go," Lisa explained desperately.

A lady came in and sat down to wait until the other had finished with Lisa. She heard what Lisa said.

"Are you one of the refugees who came in a few weeks ago?" the office manager asked as she examined her records. Lisa said that she was.

"What happened that you lost your job?" she asked

with a worried frown. Placing refugees was becoming more and more of a problem.

"I did my best, but something happened at a party and my employer fired me," Lisa told her. "'I upset a bowl of punch. I couldn't help it, but she was angry, so she let me go."

"Dear me! That's too bad," the woman said. "I don't know what to do. I'll have to find you a place to stay until something turns up."

The lady who had been waiting came to the desk.

"I'll be glad to take this young girl home with me," she said. "I came here to look for someone to work as a maid. I'll give her employment if she wishes to work for me."

Lisa took one look at her and knew that she would love this lady. The lady told the employment agent that her name was Mrs. Gray. She was small and slight, with a pleasant, attractive face. Her eyes, as they rested upon Lisa, were kind and sympathetic. For some reason Lisa felt like crying when the lady looked at her and smiled. It had been a long time since she had seen that kind look and sympathetic smile upon the face of anyone.

"I'll be glad to work for you!" she cried eagerly. "I really can work and I shall try hard to please you."

The arrangements were soon made and they left the office together. Mrs. Gray's car was parked nearby and they made their way through the traffic and out to the home where Mrs. Gray lived.

"Did I hear you say that you were a refugee from Germany?" Mrs. Gray asked.

"Yes. I was in one of Hitler's camps. Some of us escaped. My mother died there. My father was clubbed to death when Hitler's soldiers looted his store and he protested. My mother saw him die and she was never the same after that."

It seemed a relief, somehow, to unburden herself to this stranger. But the lady didn't seem like a stranger. She felt as if she were an old friend. She knew that she would love her.

"You are Jewish, aren't you?" Mrs. Gray asked. "Was that why you were in prison?"

"Yes, I am Jewish," Lisa answered.

The little gleam of light died out of her heart. She wondered if this lady felt the same way about Jews that others in Germany felt about them.

Beth Gray saw the sudden shadow across Lisa's face and she thought she knew the cause. She gave Lisa a tender smile and said, "You're a lovely Jewish girl, as pretty as I've ever seen. I shall love you more for the reason that you are a Jew. My Saviour, the Lord Jesus Christ, was a Jew, and all that we Christians have in the Word of God came to us through Jews."

Lisa stared at her in surprise. "I never heard anyone talk like that before," she said.

"We'll have lots of time to talk more about it," Beth promised. "I love to talk about it. I hope that I can help you to be happy again, for I shall do everything in my power to help you. I know what a terrible ordeal you have endured, but God is able to give you peace and to help you to forget the sorrow of the past and look with hope to the future. Not that you'll ever forget it completely, for I know that that would be impossible, but God can help you to have peace in spite of the memory."

"I don't believe there is a God," Lisa burst out bitterly. "If there is, why has He let us suffer as we have? Why didn't he save my mother and father and all of us, if we are His people?"

She regretted her outburst, but it had come involuntarily from the depths of her tortured heart.

Mrs. Gray didn't seem shocked as Lisa feared she would be. She laid her hand upon Lisa's.

"I understand just how you feel, my dear," she said gently. "I can't answer all of your questions, but perhaps I can help you to understand. We'll talk about it when you've had time to get settled and to see if you like your new job. I hope you will, for I shall love having you."

"Oh, I know I shall like it!" Lisa exclaimed. For the first time in months there was a faint smile upon her lips.

CHAPTER 13

THEY DROVE INTO THE DRIVEWAY and Lisa followed Mrs. Gray inside. The house was attractive and homey and Lisa felt that she had at last found a haven of refuge. Beth showed her to her room and Lisa uttered an exclamation of pleasure when she saw it. It was lovely, with ruffled pink curtains at the window and a pink organdy bedspread. There was a thick carpet on the floor and the furniture was of light wood, in harmony with the dainty curtains and bedspread. Lisa knew that this was no maid's room.

"This isn't a servant's room," she said. "You don't really need me as a maid, do you? Why did you offer to take me?"

"Because I was lonely and you were alone in a strange land. Isn't that reason enough? I really did want a maid, but I was doubtful of finding one who would be a companion as well as a maid. I was ill for quite a while and I'm not as strong as I once was. When I saw you and heard what you said, I was sure that the Lord had led me there at that very time."

Lisa stared at her silently. She had never heard anyone talk about God in any such manner. She couldn't understand a belief like that. Why should God concern Himself about such an insignificant thing as bringing them together when He had let so many worse things go unnoticed? If there was a God.

"I'm letting you have the guest room," Beth said. "That other room belongs to my son Glen. He's in Europe with the army. I'm praying that the war will soon be over and that he'll be coming home. I believe that God will protect him, for I've prayed earnestly that He would. He's all I have left. My other two children died when they were quite small and my husband died last year."

Lisa's mind was again filled with questioning. How could this woman be so cheerful when her only son was in danger and when she had so recently lost her husband? Why should God save this woman's son when He had let all of her own loved ones meet a terrible death? How could she have such faith in God as if He really answered prayer?

Her expression revealed something of her disturbing thoughts to Beth's keen insight.

"Suppose you let me help you put your things away," she suggested. "Then we'll have something to eat."

Lisa had only the scantiest necessities in her suitcase, for she hadn't needed many clothes and her uniforms had been furnished by Mrs. Gaynor.

She felt more contented than she thought she ever would be and the desire to live gradually grew within her, the desire which she had lost and which hadn't returned under the harsh service at Mrs. Gaynor's. Life began to mean something more than just existence, though grief still tore at her heart.

Under Beth's love and compassion the dull light left her eyes and she could smile once more, for in the atmosphere of this woman's kindness, her cheerfulness and her effort to bring sunshine into Lisa's life, Lisa couldn't fail to respond.

There was little work, with both of them working together, which Beth insisted upon, and there was ample time for conversation. Beth told Lisa about her life, of the son she adored and his plans for the future.

"He's such a fine Christian that I have no fear for him, even if he never returns," she said. "Though my heart would be broken, I know that God would give me strength to bear the pain and I would have just one more waiting for me when my time comes or when the Lord returns and I go to meet them in the air."

Lisa didn't have the slightest idea of what Beth was

talking about. Until now she had hated the name of Christian, but she loved Beth so much that her hatred of the name was fast disappearing. She longed to know more about this strange religion of hers. She wanted to know why she had such faith and what she meant by the return of the Lord.

Beth felt that it would help Lisa if she could talk about herself and she led her to tell her own life story. She had said nothing except the few words at the beginning of their acquaintance. Lisa told her about Paul and their plans to come to America, then of the tragedy that had separated them. She told her about that last moment in Paul's arms, when he had said he would wait for her, if he lived.

"I don't have much hope that he's still alive," she said as her lips trembled and tears filled her eyes. "It was like a miracle that the few of us were saved. I'm afraid he died like all the others."

"Don't give up hope, dear," Beth urged. "Just pray that God will protect him and that one day you will both see your dreams come true. I'll join you in prayer and I know that if God sees that it's best, He will answer our prayers. I know one thing, that His will is always best, even though we may not see it at the time."

"I don't pray," Lisa said dully. "What's the use? If there is a God, he's forgotten us. I don't believe any longer that there is a God."

"But there is a God, my dear," Beth said gently, "and He cares for His own. He does only what is best for those Who love Him, whether sorrow or joy, whether He answers prayer in the way we want it or not. He loves us. He loved us enough to send His Son, the Lord Jesus Christ, to die on the Cross and shed His blood, in order that we might have eternal life through Him."

"I don't believe that Jesus of Nazareth was anything but a man," Lisa said. "Our Messiah was supposed to come someday, but I stopped looking for Him long ago."

"It isn't what you believe or don't believe, Lisa,"

Beth said seriously, "but what God's Word declares. Some day I'll prove to you from your own Scriptures that Jesus Christ is the Son of God and that He is your Messiah, that He came to your people and offered Himself as your King to rule on the throne of David, and that your people refused to accept Him. He, your Messiah, has come once and one day He will come again, but He will only receive those who have believed on Him while there is yet time."

"I'll never do that," Lisa declared as the hard look crept back into her eyes. "I'll never believe in a God who has let me and my people suffer so much."

"You will, one day, my dear," and Beth put an arm around her, "because I shall be praying for you. I've been praying that you would accept Christ as your Saviour, for I know that when that happens, you'll have peace in your heart, no matter how much suffering may be there."

Lisa tried to forget what Beth had said about Jesus, but she couldn't. If Beth's belief and faith in Him as the Son of God had made her what she was, so sweet and compassionate, so gentle and considerate, so cheerful in spite of grief and loneliness and anxiety for the safety of her son, then there must be some mysterious power in this faith. Could it be possible that what she said was true? Was there really a God and was Jesus of Nazareth really His Son? Could it be that He was their Messiah and that they had rejected Him? If this were true, then all the teachings of her people were false. All that she had been taught was wrong. She was anxious to have Beth show her the proof in the sacred Scriptures of her people.

Beth had never asked Lisa to go to church with her, but one Sunday morning she did ask if she would like to go.

"Not unless I have to," Lisa told her.

"You won't ever have to go if you don't want to," Beth replied. "I'm sure that if you did go, you would enjoy the music and it would be a pleasant outing for you, if nothing more."

"Please don't ask me," Lisa begged.

When Beth left, Lisa prepared dinner so that it would

be ready when she returned, then she wandered around the house, restless and lonely, wondering what she could do to pass the time. It was the way she felt whenever Beth left her alone. She had not realized until now how much she had come to love Beth, for she seemed more like a mother than an employer.

She knew that this wonderful person had something that she didn't have, something which she couldn't understand, yet which was real, something that she wished she had, but which she felt that she never could possess. It would mean the uprooting of all her teachings, the accepting of a way of life that seemed impossible, for it would mean belief in a God whom she had denied and toward whom she felt bitterness and resentment.

She opened the door of Glen's room. She had never been in there, for Beth always cleaned it herself, carefully, as if he might come home at any moment unexpectedly. She felt like an intruder and she wondered if she was doing wrong when she went inside. It was like a shrine to the mother whose heart was over there on the battlefield with the son she adored, while her prayers hovered over him. She wondered what it must be like to have faith in prayer such as Beth had. What a comfort it must be! But what good was comfort, if her prayers weren't answered? She'd wait and see if Beth's prayers were answered about her son. How would she act if they weren't? Would she still have faith? In the meantime there was unrest and questioning in her own heart.

She saw a photograph on the table and she picked it up and looked at it closely. It was Glen in his uniform. He was a handsome young man with the same attractive eyes and features of his mother. There was the same expression in his eyes as they looked at her from the picture that she had seen that first day in Beth's eyes. Beth had said that he was a Christian. If he was like her, he must be a wonderful person. She hoped that he would escape death and bring joy to his mother's heart by returning unharmed.

She put the portrait back and closed the door. When she went into the living room she saw a book lying open upon the table. Beth didn't leave even small details of disorderliness unnoticed and Lisa wondered how it had escaped her. She didn't know that Beth had left it there on purpose, hoping that her curiosity would prompt her to read it. It was the Bible. Lisa had never seen a copy before. Beth did her reading in her room, so Lisa had never seen her reading it.

She took the Book up and began to read it casually. It had been left open at the fifty-third chapter of Isaiah, the perfect picture of prophecy of the suffering Messiah of the Jews.

Lisa read with growing interest. She read slowly the words that impressed her, even though she couldn't understand them. "He was wounded for our transgressions . . . . the Lord hath laid on him the iniquity of us all. He is brought as a lamb to the slaughter, and as a sheep before her shearers is dumb, so he openeth not his mouth."

Who is this person? Who was it who had made His grave with the wicked and the rich in His death, who was numbered with the transgressors? Was this Jesus of Nazareth? It sounded like what Beth had been talking about, yet it wasn't quite the same. She'd have to ask Beth about it.

She started to put the book down, but she saw a ribbon marker further over and she turned to it. It was the story of Christ's entry into Jerusalem when the multitudes cried Hosanna to the Son of David. Her heart began to stir within her as she read how He wept over the city, declaring that they had not known the day of their visitation. Beth had said that Jesus had offered Himself as their Messiah and King and they had rejected Him. Was this why He was weeping? Because He knew what would happen to them? Was this why they had suffered through the centuries?

She read on through the account of the crucifixion. Surely no mere man could pray for his enemies while he was suffering the torture of the spikes that were being driven through his hands. The account of His thought for His mother, charging John with her care, brought tears to her eyes. As she read the account of the resurrection and of how the Pharisees had paid the soldiers to say that the disciples had stolen His body, she wondered if it was really true that her people had believed a lie all through the centuries. What if they had been mistaken and if this Man was really their Messiah? How terrible it would be!

Then she turned to where there was another marker and read of the touching scene when Jesus met Mary, out of whom He had cast the demons, when she thought He was the gardener until He called her name in the sweetest voice she had ever heard. Lisa felt almost as if she were there in the garden kneeling at the feet of the One she had rejected herself.

She began to question more. If this man was really her Messiah, she would be among those who would suffer because of their unbelief. For the first time the thought of her own spiritual condition filled her with concern. Until now she had had no thought of anything but her desire for happiness, the things which life and the world had to offer. That was in her past life when there was happiness, before life had ceased to have any meaning for her. Now she began to wonder if, after all, there was a life beyond this one and that one must be prepared for that life by the way one lived here. Beth had told her that this was so, but she had not believed then. Now she was not so sure.

She was more disturbed than she had ever been, not about what might have happened to Paul, nor what her life would be without him, but about the soul of which she had become aware for the first time. She began to understand something of what made Beth so different from herself. It was her faith in this Jesus who claimed to be the Son of God. She must talk to Beth and try to find the answer to these disturbing questions.

When Beth returned, she found Lisa still reading, so that she didn't hear the door open. Beth greeted her and went to her room to change her clothes. There was a smile upon her lips and a glad song within her heart. Her little strategy had worked. But then it had been preceded by prayer. She knelt by the bed and thanked the Lord for the answer. She prayed that He would give the further answer that she had prayed for, that Lisa would believe that Jesus was the Son of God and that she would accept Him as her Saviour.

CHAPTER 14

BETH HOPED THAT LISA WOULD MENTION what she had been reading, but for some days Lisa said nothing about it. She wanted to ask questions, yet she hesitated, even though she was disturbed and longed to know the answers to many questions. She was reluctant to believe in Jesus as her Messiah, for she felt that she would be disloyal to her mother's religion, and though she had no faith in it herself, she disliked the thought of denying what her mother had believed. In spite of this, however, she felt a deep yearning for some kind of faith. She saw what Beth's faith gave her, how it sustained her in her anxiety about her son and in her grief over the death of her husband. If she could only have that same sustaining faith and peace where Paul was concerned. If she could only pray for his safety as Beth prayed for Glen's, she felt that she would be willing to do anything, give up anything, for that was the only thing which kept her going on, the hope that Paul was still alive and that one day they would be together again.

When the strain of waiting for some favorable news of the war and the impatience for it to end became so great that it seemed she couldn't bear it any longer, she told Beth what was on her heart.

"I hope I didn't do wrong when I read your Bible the other day," she began.

"Of course you didn't," Beth told her. "I'm glad you read it. I read it every day, for I always find comfort in its pages. It's God's Word to us, for our comfort, our instruction and our warning. Is there something you read that you'd like to talk about?"

"Do you mean that what I read were actually the words of God?" Lisa asked.

"Yes, God spoke to His prophets and apostles and they wrote what came to them through the Holy Spirit."

"It's all so mysterious. I can't understand it. I was reading of someone in the Old Testament who was killed. It said that He was led as a lamb to the slaughter and that He was wounded for our transgressions. Who was that?"

"That was Jesus, the Son of God, your Messiah," Beth said. "That was what the prophet foretold hundreds of years before Christ was born. Everything in that prophecy was fulfilled in the life and death of Jesus."

She explained in detail just how this prophecy was fulfilled, then she turned over to the passages which she thought Lisa must have been reading and related in detail the life and death of Jesus. Lisa listened with interest and a growing conviction that what she was telling her was true. But if it was true, then her people had been strangely blind not to have believed that Jesus Christ was their promised King.

"Tell me, then," she said when Beth had finished, "if God is so kind and loving and if Jesus prayed that my people would be forgiven for having Him crucified, then why did God let us suffer as we have through the centuries and even today? How can He be a loving Father and then allow us to suffer so?"

"Because your people rejected His Son," Beth said sadly. "God is merciful and loving and compassionate, but He is also just. He gave your people His word in centuries past and He chose the descendants of Abraham as His peculiar people, so that through them His Son should be born to be the Saviour of the world. He warned them time and again that if they rejected Him and worshiped idols, He would cast them off and scatter them throughout the world."

"But that was hundreds of years ago. Why must we suffer because they sinned?" Lisa asked.

"Because when Jesus stood before Pilate, the Roman

governor, to be tried for His life, Pilate found no fault in
Him and he told the people so. They cried out that if Pilate
didn't have Him crucified, he was no friend of Caesar's.
Pilate was afraid he would lose his office as Governor if
he refused to have Jesus crucified, so he took a basin of
water and washed his hands and said, 'I am innocent of the
blood of this just person.' The Jews cried, 'Let His blood
be on us and our children.' When they uttered those words
they brought down upon them and their children the punishment that has been theirs even until today."

"And still you say that He is a merciful God?"

"Yes, my dear, for today your people have the same
opportunity to receive forgiveness for their sins that we
Gentiles have. If they come to God in faith and accept
His Son as their Saviour, He will protect them and bless
them the same way He does us. Many Jews have accepted
Christ and they have the same peace that I have in my
heart. You can have that same peace, Lisa dear, if you
will only believe."

Lisa shook her head. "I wish I could, but there is too
much hate in my heart," she said sadly. "If your son
comes home safely, I may be able to believe that God answers prayer."

"You can't bargain with God, dear. You either acknowledge that you are a sinner who needs a Saviour
and open your heart to the gift of eternal life or you will
never believe. You don't just believe because He might
answer my prayer or doubt if He doesn't. I'd still love
Him and have faith in His love if I never saw my son again.
Think this over, Lisa, and try to believe. You could, if
you'd only ask God for the faith to believe."

She went to her desk and got out a little Bible.

"Read this and try to believe what it says. I shall
pray that God will soon open your heart to the truth and
that one day you will know the peace that only God can
give."

Lisa took the Book but she didn't promise to read it.
She didn't want to read it because it disturbed her too

much and she had enough to disturb her without adding any more.

Not long after this the news burst upon the world that the Normandy invasion had been accomplished and that Hitler was battling for his existence. The allied armies were blasting their way toward Berlin and thousands were being slaughtered on both sides while the war was being fought to its close.

The world was electrified and read every bit of news that came through. Those who had loved ones in the thick of the fight lived through days filled with anxiety and torment, wondering what the end would be for them.

Lisa saw the serious light in Beth's eyes, though she went about the daily tasks with a smile and always seemed cheerful when they were together, but sometimes when Beth was in her room, Lisa could hear her pouring out her petitions to God for the safety of her son. After Lisa had gone to bed, she could hear Beth praying and occasionally she heard her sobbing as she prayed. She wished she could pray this way for Paul, but there was a hardness in her heart that was like a wall, hindering her. She remembered that Beth had said that God only promised to undertake for His children, those who loved Him and had been redeemed by the blood of His Son. Since she didn't love Him and didn't believe, there was no use praying. She felt rebellious and sad at the same time. She felt that she had been left out, alone and forsaken in a world where there was no hope.

Beth had told her how she might be taken in where she could feel safe and sure of God's love and care for her life, but her stubborn will and bitterness made her refuse to open the door and let Him in. In spite of what Beth had said, she decided that she would wait and see if God answered her prayers for Glen's return. If he came home, then she might try to believe. If he didn't, then she would know that she had been right, that God didn't care and didn't answer prayer.

As the days dragged on while those at home waited and

hoped and prayed, Lisa also waited with little hope that Paul had lived through all the horror and carnage.

When at last Hitler was forced to flee from those he had sought to conquer and news of victory was flashed to a waiting world, still there was anxiety in many hearts. How many would come back alive? Lisa waited as anxiously as Beth did for some word from Glen, but no word came.

It took weeks and sometimes months before some of those at home knew what had happened to their loved ones. Those who were wounded most severely were sent home first, then later others followed.

Lisa began to fear that Beth would never see her son again, for Christmas was almost at hand and there still was no word from him. Beth, however, didn't give up hope. She still waited and prayed, though Lisa could see that the strain was telling on her. She looked thin and worn and her effort to be cheerful became more apparent.

Neither of them cared to make any preparation to celebrate the day. It meant nothing to Lisa, for she had never celebrated it, since her people didn't recognize Christ's birthday as a time for celebration. Beth did bake fruit cake and bought several gifts. She bought gifts for Glen and wrapped them carefully in bright paper and ribbon.

"I'll have them ready just in case he comes," she told Lisa. "I still feel that he'll be here before long. These candies are his favorites. He'll have his Christmas whenever he comes."

Lisa's heart ached for her, for she felt that Glen was long since dead.

On Christmas Eve, just as Beth was turning out the lights, she heard a car stop at the door and she went to see who it was. A young soldier came up the walk as the taxi drove away. Beth uttered a glad cry and in a few moments she was in Glen's arms while she wept for joy on his shoulder. They came into the house together and Beth's face was radiant through her tears.

"He's back, Lisa!" she cried. "He's come home at last. God has answered my prayers."

Lisa came out of her room and stood looking at the two with their arms around each other. Beth introduced them and explained briefly why Lisa was there. As Glen acknowledged the introduction, Lisa saw his eyes fastened upon her with the look she had seen so often in the eyes of others and it brought a little feeling of warmth to her. She knew she would like this handsome young soldier and she hoped that he would like her. Life would be more interesting while she waited, now that he was here.

"Let's sit down and talk for a while, even though I know you're tired," Beth suggested. "You stay with us, Lisa," she urged as Lisa started to leave.

"I hoped for some word from you before the invasion," Beth said as Lisa joined them.

"There wasn't time for anything but fighting and hoping that we wouldn't be the next ones to be blown to bits," Glen told her. "I was in the hospital during the last week of fighting. I'm still under doctor's orders to report for a checkup every now and then. They were afraid of TB, but I think I escaped that."

They talked for a while and Beth asked him about the war but he was reluctant to talk about it. The horror of it was too fresh in his mind.

Early the next morning Glen was up and his mother heard him stirring, so she got up and dressed. They went into the kitchen while she made coffee. He asked her about Lisa and she told him what she knew, of the tragedy that had come to her and of her determination to find out whether Paul was still alive. She told him how she had witnessed to her and of her hope that one day she would accept Christ as her Saviour.

"She said that if you returned, she would try to believe that God answered prayer," Beth told him. "Now I shall have something to work on. You are the living proof that He does answer prayer." She patted Glen's head as she bent over him, then she kissed him on his thin cheek. "How thankful I am for the answer!"

"I'm afraid that her hopes of finding her sweetheart are pretty slim," he said. "Mighty few of those camps had anyone alive in them when our men reached them. Hitler had ordered them to be emptied before we reached them and they were slaughtered like animals. God will surely punish that demon-possessed beast for what he has done to the Jews, if for nothing else."

"Yes, the promise and the warning still hold true that God gave to Abraham," Beth remarked. "He will bless those who bless them and punish those who persecute them."

"Lisa's the prettiest thing I've seen in a long time," Glen said. "It's been so long since I've even talked to a girl that I scarcely know what to say."

Lisa came in soon, offering to help Beth finish the breakfast, but Beth protested.

"We're ahead of time," she said. "Neither of us could sleep for joy, so we got up. I almost forgot that today is Christmas. What a Christmas this will be! I've had the best Christmas present that I could ever hope to have."

After breakfast they went into the living room and opened their packages. Glen was surprised when his mother handed his to him.

"I surely didn't expect anything," he told her. "I wasn't even thinking about Christmas. I was just remembering that I was on my way home and that I'd soon be seeing you."

"I prepared, so that if you did get here, you would have them. I knew they would keep until you did come."

"You never gave up hope that I would return, did you?"

"No, though at times I'll confess that my faith was weak. How glad I am that I still kept my faith and still prayed."

Lisa remembered what she had said. God had answered prayer. Glen was at home. If she could believe, perhaps she could pray and God would answer her prayers. But could she believe? Beth said that a person couldn't bargain with God, that there must be a genuine desire to ask for forgiveness and to believe that Jesus would give the gift of eternal life. Could she believe? Could she erase the bitterness and unbelief from her heart? She would have to talk to Beth about it again.

She envied Beth in her happiness. Would she ever know such happiness again? She longed to have Beth's faith. But there was still no faith within her and small hope.

CHAPTER 15

FOR THE FIRST TIME since her dreams were shattered, Lisa began to take an interest in life. Even under the influence of Beth's friendship, her kindness and her effort to help Lisa feel more cheerful, she had failed to respond. Lisa had seemed to be living for only one thing, to be able to get back and find out about Paul.

Beth had spoken to her friends about Lisa and had asked their prayers for her. They had all sympathized with the girl and had prayed that one day soon the hate and bitterness would melt under the power of the Holy Spirit and that she would know the joy of the Lord as they knew it.

When Glen returned, life began to change for Lisa. At first the boy was worn and weak and remained in bed for the greater part of the day, as his doctor had recommended, but as his strength returned he brought the cheerfulness and the radiance of youth into the lives of all of them. Beth went about her work singing the songs she hadn't been able to sing until now. Sometimes Glen joined her and their voices rang out as Beth worked and Glen watched her.

The affection between mother and son brought back memories to Lisa of her own parents and their love for her, memories that caused such heartache that sometimes she had to go to her room and weep there.

Glen noticed this and knew that she had been crying. He longed to be able to comfort her, so he would begin telling her stories of the laughable things that had happened when he first went across, trying to make her smile.

She knew what he was trying to do and it made her like him more because of his sympathy. When she asked him questions about the more serious and tragic side of the war, he was still reluctant to talk about what had happened.

"I want to forget that terrible time," he told her, "but I'm afraid I never can. I wake at night and see some of it all over again. I see the mangled bodies lying out there, torn to bits by shells, or else hear someone screaming in the agony of death, knowing that there is nothing I can do for him. Then I see some young fellow not as old as I am trying to hold down a position against us, which he has been commanded to hold at all costs, and I'm forced to shoot him down. Then I wonder if he has ever had a chance to know the Lord, or if I've sent a soul out into a Christless eternity. It's a terrible thought and I felt for a while that I couldn't stand it. It seemed impossible for me to fire a shot. Then when I was at a gun emplacement, the horror of it all overcame me. I had the wild desire to run away from it all, not because I was afraid for my own life, but I couldn't bear the thought of those I would be killing, young men with all of life before them who had to be cut down without ever having had a chance to know the Lord. That's why I don't want to talk about it. I couldn't even tell this to Mother, even though I know she'd understand."

"Do you mean that you didn't hate those Nazis who were torturing us and who were trying to destroy the world?" she asked in surprise.

"I can't have hate in my heart while the love of God is there," he said. "I hate the sin which led them into this war and I hate the sin of that madman who was responsible for it all, but I couldn't hate those who were the victims of his mad scheme. Sin made them what they were. If they had had the same chance that I had under my mother's teachings, they might have had the same love in their hearts that I have in mine and this war would never have been started. Even Hitler would have been different if he had had the opportunity to know the Lord."

"I can't understand such an attitude," she said. "I

hate them all. Perhaps you would, too, if you had suffered as my people have suffered and if your parents had
died as mine died. I would have enjoyed killing Hitler with
my bare hands."

"I understand how you feel," he said sympathetically,
"and I don't blame you, because you don't know what it
means to have the love of God in your heart. Jesus said to
love your enemies, to bless them that curse you, to do
good to them that hate you and to pray for them that persecute you. That seems impossible and it would be if we
tried this by ourselves, but when we have the strength
of Christ within us, it's not impossible. But I'll confess
that still it isn't easy."

"Do you mean that you could love Hitler?" she asked.

He smiled. "That's a hard question to answer. I
hate what the man stood for and the motives which inspired him. I hated what he was doing, but I felt sorry for
him, because I knew what a terrible punishment he faced.
That's as near an answer as I can give. I'm not perfect,
believe me. I'm only trying to grow in grace. I suppose
you think I'm a weakling and not a very good soldier," he
said as he saw her serious eyes appraising him.

"I think you're wonderful," she exclaimed while her
eyes glowed. "You're like your mother and she is the most
wonderful person I've ever known. She lives what she pro-
fesses and she makes me want to live as she lives. I wish
I had what she has."

Sadness crept into her eyes and a faint sigh escaped her.

"If Mom didn't have the love of God in her heart, she
wouldn't have any more than you have," he said seriously.
"You see, we were sinners once and lost souls, but when
we came to the Lord and asked Him to forgive and to save,
He heard our petition and He saved us. We were born
again because we had a new nature. We not only had
physical life which we received when we were born into
the world, but we had eternal life which the Lord gave us
when He forgave our sins and saved us from their penalty.
And now we have the peace of God within our hearts

which makes Mom like she is. It's all simple, yet wonderful."

"It's simple when you can believe, but it's difficult when you don't believe."

"You could believe, if you only would," he stated emphatically.

"You don't understand," and she shook her head. "All my life I have been taught that Jesus was only a man who claimed to be something He wasn't. I tried to believe in God as my parents did, but I never saw Him answer prayer and when sorrow came, I grew to hate Him. Then I stopped believing that there was a God. I don't think He would ever forgive me because my heart is still full of hate and bitterness and unbelief."

"My heart aches for you, for I know what you must suffer. You suffer more because you're bearing it all alone. I had my share of sorrow out there alone at night, when I thought that perhaps I'd never see Mom again and when news came about my father's death. I couldn't have borne it in my own strength, but I had the sustaining power and comfort that only God can give and I had the peace that came from Him, even while I was burdened with my grief and about the killing that I was forced to do. Let me help you, won't you? I won't try to persuade you any more, but I'll join Mom in praying for you, that you'll one day be happy again and that your heart's desire will be granted to you."

"You're kind," Lisa murmured. "I'll never be able to repay you and your mother for what both of you mean to me and what you're doing to make life bearable again."

There were tears in her eyes, and to Glen she looked lovely. In this short time he felt himself becoming more and more attracted to her. He didn't want that to happen for many reasons. He knew that her one desire was to find Paul and that there could be no place in her heart for anyone as long as there was hope that he might be alive. Then, she was not a believer and she had hardened her heart against the pleading of the Holy Spirit. Only a miracle could melt that hardness and leave the way open for her salvation. No matter how beautiful she was, nor how she attracted him, he must not fall in love with her. It could bring nothing but unhappiness.

Beth noticed her son's interest in Lisa and was afraid. She not only prayed about it but she spoke to Glen one day.

"Glen, I know how lovely Lisa is," she began, "and how attractive she must be to any young man, but don't let her beauty lead you into something which will only bring you heartache."

Glen uttered a self-conscious little laugh and hugged his mother.

"Still watching me and forgetting that I'm a man now, not your headstrong little boy, always getting into a mess and looking to you to get him out."

"I'm trying to save you before you get into a mess," she retorted. "Even if Lisa were a Christian, she's in love with someone else. She'll never love anyone else as long as she hopes to find him again. She's just living for the day when she can go back to look for him."

"I know that, Mother," he said, "and I'm not falling in love with her. I like her and I admire her beauty, but I realize that there are many barriers."

Then he gave her a kiss. "I'm off tomorrow to town to look for a job. Mr. Horton promised me before I left that he'd take me into his law firm when I came back. He might have been thinking that the chances against me were so good that he'd be safe in offering me the job. I'll see if he's a man of his word. I'll either give him a surprise or a big disappointment. I'm afraid I've forgotten what I've learned."

"You'll get the job," she assured him. "He knows you're back and he told me when I was in town that you could start whenever you were strong enough."

"So you even fixed that up for your little boy. I wonder what I'd do without you."

When he went to town he found that Mr. Horton was expecting him. He told Glen about his mother's visit.

"She still thinks that I'm a little boy and that she has to take care of me," Glen said. "It's rather embarrassing sometimes, but I love her for her interest in me. I hope that I can prove to you that I can stand on my own two feet now."

"I'm sure that any young soldier who has won the purple heart and a citation for meritorious service under fire can stand upon his own two feet in the practice of law," Mr. Horton replied.

"How did you know that?" Glen asked in surprise. "I haven't even told my mother about that. I told her that I was sick, but I didn't tell her that it was because I returned to duty too soon after I was wounded. I can't feel too proud of the citation because it meant so many I had killed."

"A neighbor's boy who was in your same detachment told me," Mr. Horton said seriously. "Don't let the thought of those killings get you down. Killing in war is terrible, I'll admit, but in war it is doing your duty to save your country and you surely were doing your part when the whole world was in danger. Killing in war when there is no hatred in a soldier's heart for an individual, isn't the same as murder."

"I understand," Glen told him, "but still I didn't want to boast of something which had cost so many lives."

Mr. Horton looked at the handsome young man and pain tore at his heart. He was thinking of his own son who didn't come back. He would have been in Glen's place, but he had been among the first casualties before Glen even went across.

"I'll be happy to have you work with me," Mr. Horton said. "Suppose you begin at once. I have some claims for you to investigate. Come with me and I'll show you your office and where to begin."

Glen was elated. He had not only come home alive and well, but there was security for the future. How good the Lord was! He offered a silent prayer of thanks as he followed Mr. Horton to what was to be his office.

While Beth went out to call on some neighbors, Lisa remained at home alone. She thought about what Glen had so recently told her about his faith and what it meant to him. She tried to understand a love like that which he described, a love which so filled his heart that there was no room for hatred, not even for Hitler.

She couldn't believe that it could be real. Yet something dominated his life, the same force that controlled the life of his mother. It must be something real or the results wouldn't be the same in both their lives. It couldn't be pretense. It was deep and abiding. She longed for it more than ever. She longed for anything that would ease the gnawing pain in her heart, the agonizing impatience to go back to where Paul had said he would be waiting for her. But what was the use of longing for something that she could never possess?

CHAPTER 16

WHEN GLEN STARTED TO WORK Lisa missed him. She hadn't realized how much his presence had meant to her until he was no longer there all day. He was enthused and happy in his work. Though it had been several years since he had been to law school, he found that he could adjust himself with surprising success. He would have to study at night in order to finish his law course, but in the meantime he was getting the practical side of the work. He had little time to spend with Lisa and he was glad, for he found that, in spite of his resolutions, he was growing to love her. Often, at work, when he should have been thinking of the work before him, he let his thoughts wander to her, her lovely face with the eyes which held such sorrow when she thought no one was looking, yet which lighted up so suddenly when he talked to her, and he knew that he was near to loving her.

He wondered what she would do when she was able to return to Europe, if she should learn that Paul was no longer alive. He wondered if she would return to America, or if she would prefer to remain where she had always lived. He knew how she would suffer if she found that her hopes were destroyed and that the boy she loved was no longer alive.

He knew that only the grace of God could sustain her, yet he feared that she would never receive that grace.

If she should return to America and if she could accept Christ as her Saviour, then perhaps he could try to win her. But that was wishful thinking and would perhaps lead nowhere.

As time passed, in spite of all he had said to himself and to his mother, he knew that he loved her. He was worried about it, but he knew that worrying wouldn't help, so he tried to forget it. He discovered that forgetting was not easy. In fact it seemed impossible.

Lisa looked forward to evenings he was free to spend with her. Glen loved to see the light in Lisa's eyes when they talked, for she hung upon his words with an interest that inspired him and pleased him while it thrilled his heart.

Beth saw with growing concern what was happening to Glen and she prayed about it, but she said nothing more to him, for she knew that talking wouldn't help.

Lisa seemed completely unaware of Glen's love. She liked him and enjoyed being with him, but beyond that she didn't seem to notice what was so plain to Beth's anxious eyes.

There was a young girl, Lotta Sherwood, who had known Glen all her life and who had been his constant companion before he had left for Europe, but since his return he hadn't even phoned her. Beth was hoping that they would renew their relationship, for she knew how Lotta felt toward Glen. She hadn't tried to hide it. Lotta was a Christian and Beth was sure that she would make Glen happy. She asked him one evening about Lotta.

"You never have phoned her since you came home and it's been ages now," Beth said. "I'm sure she must feel hurt at your neglect. Aren't you interested in her any longer?"

"I'd forgotten all about her," Glen admitted. "So much has happened since I went away and I've had other things on my mind."

Beth guessed what those "other things" were.

"She thought a great deal of you," Beth continued. "I'm sure she wonders why you've neglected her."

"What do you mean by that, Mom?" he asked a little irritably. "She doesn't have any claim on me, so I've not neglected her."

"Even though you forgot her, she never forgot you. She never failed to ask me about you every time we met at church and when the invasion began, she always mentioned your name in our prayer meeting. I'm sure she cares for you, Glen. Don't hurt her. Phone her and get in touch with her, won't you?"

Glen cast a reproving eye upon his mother. He knew why she mentioned Lotta. It was for Lisa's benefit.

Lisa spoke before he replied. "It would be nice to know her. If she likes you, I'm sure that I would like her. Perhaps she would be a friend, if she wouldn't be prejudiced against me because I'm Jewish."

"She's a Christian, dear," Beth told her. "She would like you and she wouldn't be prejudiced against you for the same reason I wasn't."

"You're different from other Christians," Lisa said while the hard light crept into her eyes. "Those who tortured us called themselves Christians. I used to hate the name until I met you."

"They were not Christians, Lisa," Beth explained. "They were only Gentiles. If they had been Christians, they never could have persecuted your people. They would have had a compassion for them because their Saviour was a Jew and because He promised a blessing upon those who love His brethren in the flesh."

"I never knew there was any difference until I met you," Lisa confessed.

"Suppose I invite Lotta over some evening for dinner," Beth suggested, with her eyes upon Glen.

Glen shrugged his shoulders and said nothing.

When Lotta came Beth's heart ached for the girl. She tried valiantly not to show her feeling for Glen, but it showed in her eyes as she looked at him. Glen was embarrassed and scarcely knew what to say. He felt guilty, for he knew that it was because he had been so absorbed with Lisa that he hadn't even wanted to call her.

"It's been a long time since I've had a chance to talk to you," Lotta said. "When I saw you in church, you were so far away that I couldn't even get near you to welcome you home. You hurried out before I could reach you."

"I've been pretty busy," Glen explained lamely. "I went to work as soon as I was strong enough and I've been studying quite hard ever since."

When Lotta was introduced to Lisa, Beth was surprised at her attitude. The smile left her face and she gave Lisa such a cool greeting that Beth was amazed. She feared that all the assurance she had given Lisa about Lotta would prove false. She suspected why Lotta was so cool, but that didn't excuse her rudeness. She saw how beautiful Lisa was and her jealousy made her afraid that Glen was interested in Lisa.

She looked Lisa over unsmilingly and said, "I heard about you when you first came to work for Mrs. Gray."

Beth hastened to intervene. "Lisa is one of the family," she explained. "She has suffered much from Hitler's cruelty and we're trying to make her forget and be happy again."

Lisa said nothing, but Beth could see the cold hate in her eyes as they rested upon Lotta. Lisa was sure that this girl would never be her friend and she didn't want her for a friend. She was like all the others. She was just a Gentile who despised the Jew.

The conversation was strained during Lotta's visit and when she finally left, all three of them were relieved. Lisa turned to Beth.

"She's no different from the others and I hate her like all the others."

"Perhaps some day you'll understand why she acted that way," Beth told her.

She couldn't tell Lisa what she suspected as the reason for the way Lotta had acted. Even if her suspicions were correct, it was no excuse for the girl's surprising rudeness. She went to her room and left the two alone.

"I'm disappointed in her," Lisa remarked. "I had hoped that she would be my friend. I don't have any friends here except your mother and you."

"Mom didn't know all the truth about Lotta," he said.

"She didn't know that before I went away, Lotta told me that she loved me. I thought then that I was in love with her. Many of the fellows did foolish things just before they went across. They married and regretted it before long. I told Lotta that I wanted to wait until I came home, for I didn't know what might happen to me. There was no definite engagement and I told her that I wouldn't write. That's why she never heard from me except through Mother. I don't feel that I've done wrong by not getting in touch with her since I came home. I thought she would understand that I had changed. Mom didn't know this and I didn't want to tell her. I wish I had, for then this would never have happened and you wouldn't have been hurt by her rudeness. She surely didn't give a very good testimony as a Christian."

"I think I understand why she didn't like me," Lisa said. "She thinks that I'm in love with you and that you might be interested in me."

"She knows that I'm in love with you," he corrected. "I'm sure she saw what you've never seen, Lisa, that I love you. I didn't want to love you, for I know that your heart belongs to Paul, but I couldn't help it. I love you very much. I tried not to, but I do."

He hadn't meant to say it, but it was out. He was sorry, for he had made brave resolutions and now they had been destroyed. He was ashamed of his weakness, for he was afraid that his confession would only cause hurt to her, and he knew that she didn't love him.

Lisa looked at him while tears slowly filled her eyes. Her lips trembled as she tried to keep her voice steady.

"I never dreamed that you could love me like that," she stammered. "I never thought that anyone over here could love me like that. I just thought that you felt sorry for me and you were being kind because you knew how I had suffered. It's—it's too wonderful to believe."

He was surprised at her reaction, but then he thought he understood. He tried to put himself in her place, in a land where she was a stranger and an alien, belonging to a race that had been despised and persecuted, feeling forsaken by God and man. To have it revealed to her that someone really loved her for herself and was not just being kind, was a revelation.

He gave her a smile, "At first I did feel sorry for you and was just being kind. But after I got to know you I couldn't help but fall in love with you. My prayers for you will always be that you may have the happiness you long for, and that one day you will learn to love the Lord as I love Him and that you will let Him take care of you as only He can."

"You're not asking anything of me, not even my love?" she asked in surprise.

"Why should I ask?" he replied sadly. "I know that your heart belongs to Paul. I wouldn't dare try to persuade you to try to forget him and to love me, because I don't believe that I could. It would make me happy if I could, but I know that you're living for only one thing, to find him again."

"That's true," she said. "I've loved Paul for so long that loving him is a part of my very life. All I live for is the hope of finding him alive. You're so wonderful! I can't put into words what I feel toward you. There's a love in my heart that's different from any I've ever had, though it isn't the love that you would ask for. It's different from the love I have for your mother. She is only being kind to me because she knows that I am lonely and heartbroken and that I need her. I shall always carry this love for you in my heart, no matter what happens to me. You even make me want to be a Christian," she admitted with a faint smile.

"That's what I want above everything," he said fervently, "even more than I want your love, for it will mean more to you, not only now, but through all eternity."

"I shall try hard to believe," she promised.

"If you would try to pray for faith instead of just trying to believe, I know that you would believe," he urged. "If you would ask God to give you faith, I know He would."

"How can I pray to God, when I don't even believe in Him?" she asked.

"You know there is a God, in spite of your claim that you don't believe He exists. You've said that both Mom and I have something that you wish you had. Well, it's our belief in the God who is also your God that makes us what we are. He has given us what we have and He can give you what you want, if you'd only trust Him and ask Him."

She shook her head. "I wish I could, but I just can't."

"Tell me," he said, changing the subject, "what will you do if you get back home and you're convinced that Paul is dead?"

"I shall want to die," she told him. "I shall feel like killing myself. There will be nothing left to live for. I wouldn't want to live."

"But you would," he assured her. "You're young and your whole life is before you. You can still be happy, even if you pass through that sorrow."

"I can't believe that," she sighed. "I'm no longer a child. I'm a woman now and sometimes I feel old, weighed down by sorrow. It seems so long since the day Paul and I planned our wedding day. The years since then seem like eternities."

"Promise me one thing," he begged. "If you get back and if you find out that Paul is dead, come back and make your home here."

"I can't promise. Once I get over there, I may not be able to come back. Let's wait and see what happens."

"There will be a problem about your going back," he admitted. "There will be the question about your passport in the event that you do want to return. You're a refugee, you see, not just an immigrant admitted under the quota. I don't know just what the procedure will be, but I'll look into it and try to get everything arranged for you."

"You're kind to do this for me and not ask for anything in return," she said.

"I do ask for something in return," he contradicted. "I ask you to promise to come back here if the one you seek is no longer alive."

"If I get there, that is all I want," she maintained. "After that, no matter what I find, nothing else matters."

"It matters to me," he said gently. "If he is no longer there, you will need someone to help you go on with life. You'll need Mom and me. I want to be the one who will help you want to live. That's all I ask."

"If anyone could make me want to live if Paul is dead, it would have to be you," she told him.

CHAPTER 17

LISA WAITED WITH GROWING IMPATIENCE and anxiety, while a war-torn world was trying to be adjusted to peace, while heart-broken mothers and wives and sweethearts endeavored to adjust themselves to desolate homes and blasted hopes.

Glen investigated the situation that involved Lisa. He knew that it would perhaps be difficult to get her status cleared and to obtain passports that would allow her to return if she wanted to. He was determined to have this arrangement made, if possible, not for his own sake alone, but for hers. If she should return home and should find Paul and her friends gone, there would be no reason for her to remain.

Lisa had written to Greda and asked about Paul, but in the confusion after the war, if the letter was ever received, there was no answer, and as time passed, she didn't write again. She admitted to herself that she feared she might learn that Paul was dead and she wanted to put off that evil news as long as possible. It was better to keep on hoping.

As the weeks dragged by, however, she became afraid that if Paul was alive and was waiting for her, he might think that she was dead. If he thought that, then he might leave and she would never find him.

One evening when Glen came home and his mother was out, he sat in the living room reading. He thought that Lisa was out also until he heard the sound of sobbing, and realized it was coming from Lisa's room. He went to the door and knocked. The sobs ceased and soon she opened the door and looked at him through tear-drenched eyes.

"What's happened?" he asked anxiously.

"Nothing," she replied, "but I'm so tired of waiting. I don't believe I'll ever get back home."

"You won't have to wait much longer," he promised after he had led her into the living room. "I've been working on your case and Mr. Horton has been a big help. We hope that before long the necessary papers will come through. Surely the Lord has had a hand in this, for Mr. Horton has a friend in the immigration department in Washington and he has been corresponding with this man ever since I asked him to help me with your problem. He had a letter this afternoon, saying that perhaps in a few weeks the way will be clear for you to go back. Doesn't that make you happy?"

"Yes, it does," and she smiled through her tears. "I believe I have enough saved up for my passage across. Your mother has been generous and I've saved every penny that I could."

"How about the passage back?" he asked.

"I don't have enough for that."

"Then I'll let you have it."

"I couldn't take it," she objected. "Your mother has paid me far more than I earned. Both of you have been so kind that I couldn't ask for anything more. I'll be satisfied just to get back."

"We'll call it a loan, but I shall insist that you take enough to keep you while you're over there and to bring you back when you're ready to come. Didn't you tell me that you and Paul had planned to come to America? Well, if he's still waiting for you and if he still wants to come, you'll have enough so that both of you can come back and begin life all over again here."

"You would want that?" she asked. She couldn't understand such unselfishness.

"I would want even that," he assured her. "I love you enough to want your happiness above everything. It's true that I want you myself, but, if that can't be, I shall know that, in God's will, it's for the best. You see, I believe what God says in His Word, that all things work together for good to those who love the Lord. I believe that if I can't have you, He has something else in store for me. I can't imagine what it could possibly be, but I believe it's true. So you can take the money as a loan and when you and Paul are able, you can repay me and I'll be happy to know that I've had a part in making you happy."

"I can't understand a love like that," she murmured, but her eyes were shining.

"You will, when you understand what it means to be a Christian," he assured her.

"You make me want to be one."

"Then do something for me. Go to church with me Sunday."

She couldn't refuse though she wanted to. She dreaded meeting the strangers who might treat her as coldly as Lotta had done, and there was still that little lump of hardness and bitterness within her that rebelled against anything pertaining to the Christ she still rejected.

"I promise," she told him.

"You've made me happy," he said, "and I somehow feel that in the end this will be the means of making you happy, too."

That evening Glen told his mother that Lisa had promised to go to church with him. Beth tried to look pleased, but he saw the worry in her eyes.

"Don't be worried about me, Mom," he said. "I love her and I've told her so, but we both know that I can never have her, so I'm not shedding any tears about it. She'll soon be going back home to look for Paul. I'm glad to have had a part in making her happy. If I can't have her, perhaps God will give me someone else to take her place. Now can you give me a smile?"

"God has been good to give me such a wonderful son," she said in husky tones. "I know that whatever He does for you will be for your good, for I know that you're His child and in His will."

Lisa dreaded the ordeal of going to church, but when she finally entered the building and took her place between Glen and his mother, she felt the spirit of reverence steal over her and her dread vanished. She felt that she was in a house of worship and her own spirit seemed to feel a reverence which she had never felt in her services in the synagogue.

When she and her parents had gone occasionally to the synagogue in the nearby town, she had had no feeling but a sense of duty. The prayers and rituals were meaningless to her. They meant nothing, for there was no inspiration in them. The rabbi seemed to be praying words which were meaningless to a Being who wasn't near, who was far off and who probably wasn't even listening.

When the minister came in and knelt in prayer, she saw the others bow their heads while they joined in prayer and, though no word was audible, she felt that somehow these prayers were reaching out to the God they worshiped.

The minister announced a hymn and the congregation sang with radiant faces and a joy that seemed to emanate from within. These songs had a message, though she wondered about them. There was much emphasis upon blood.

Then she remembered the sacrifices which her people had offered in past centuries when there was a priest and an altar. She heard them singing "Look to the Lamb of God," and she thought that she understood. Beth had tried to explain to her that Jesus was the Lamb of God and that all of their sacrifices in the past had looked forward to the time when the Lamb of God should shed His blood for the sins of the world. She hadn't even tried to understand then, but now she thought she did. These people were singing about Jesus as if He were their sacrifice.

The minister's sermon verified this. He was preaching on the atoning power of the blood of Christ, saying that without it there was no salvation and that through it, every sin could be forgiven and the sinner would no longer be under the condemnation for sin.

As she listened, she began to understand that this was true and she had to admit what she had so long refused to believe, that Jesus Christ must indeed be the Son of God and that God was real. As she continued to listen with absorbed interest, God seemed especially real to her. She felt under such condemnation for her years of unbelief and hatred that she could scarcely keep the tears back.

She was thinking of herself in the light of Calvary and of her own spiritual need, not of her suffering heart, and she longed for the peace about which the minister was speaking.

What a terrible thing her people had done if this minister was right. They had crucified their promised Messiah. She could no longer doubt this fact, for she heard what the Bible was proclaiming as the minister read different passages from it to prove his point. The facts were too manifest, even to her untaught mind.

When the sermon was ended, she felt that she would like to go forward with the others who went down the aisle and knelt at the altar to accept Christ as Saviour, but she was afraid to go. There was a weight upon her heart, the weight of a great longing as well as the weight of the knowledge of her own sin and need.

When they were in the car on their way home, she told Beth how she felt, that she had wanted to accept Christ.

"How I wish you had!" Beth exclaimed. "Our minister has been praying about you, for I told him of your need and how you wanted to believe."

"I do want to," Lisa told her. "I want to more than anything in the world. I'm sorry that I was so stubborn and unbelieving. I know now that I've been wrong all this time."

"Then you do believe that there is a God and that He loves you?" Beth asked.

"I believe that Jesus Christ is God's Son and that He really is our Messiah," she said reverently.

"How glad I am to hear you say that!" Beth exclaimed. "Then are you willing to ask Him to forgive you and to save your soul? If you are, you can do that right here."

"You mean that I don't have to wait to go down to the altar? I think I would be willing to go another time."

"There's no time like the present," Beth said. "You can accept Christ as your Saviour right now, if you will."

"Then I will," Lisa said.

They bowed their heads and Beth prayed with her. Then she told Lisa how to pray and when they raised their heads again, there was a new sense of peace in Lisa's heart, as if a great weight had been lifted.

"Now I think I can want to live, even if I never find Paul," she said as she wiped her eyes.

In the front seat Glen was praying while he drove. He was thanking God that he had been used to water the seed that his mother had already planted in Lisa's heart, that he had added the final little touch when he had asked her to go to church with him. He prayed that he might have the strength he would need when Lisa left, perhaps never to return. He also prayed that he might be subject to God's will and that if he could never have Lisa, he might be the better for having loved her.

CHAPTER 18

LISA WAS STILL CONFUSED in her thinking. There had come into her heart a peace that she had never known before, but, now that she had found this peace, other thoughts gave her concern. Though the bitterness she had felt toward God had disappeared while a new reverence for Him took its place in her heart, there was still bitterness over the tragedy which had overwhelmed her and it still rankled within her heart. There was still hatred of Hitler and those who had been used by him to torture and kill her loved ones.

She knew that this should not be and it worried her. If, as Beth expressed it, she was really born again, she shouldn't have this in her heart. Beth had said that where there was the love of God, there was no room for hatred. She must ask Beth about it. At the first opportunity she did. Beth tried to explain it to her.

"When we have received this spiritual new birth, we are what the Apostle Paul calls babes in Christ. Just as a baby has to learn to walk, so the babe in Christ has to learn to walk in the new way of life. Self, which is this old nature of ours, has to be conquered and we have to gain victory over all of our faults. We can't do this all at once and we can't do it in our own power, so we have to lean upon the Lord and depend upon Him to help us to be victorious."

"I don't know what you mean by leaning on the Lord," Lisa said. "I thought everything wrong in my heart would be taken away at once."

"I mean that you must pray that He will give you strength to overcome. His Holy Spirit gives us the power when we pray and ask for that power," Beth explained. "The Christian life isn't an easy one and those who promise that it will be make a grave mistake in telling that to young Christians. It is a constant battle against temptation that Satan puts in our way. Paul says that we fight against the powers of evil all about us. We have to put on the armor of God. I'll show you that in Corinthians and we'll talk about it later, but the first and most necessary thing is prayer, with faith."

"If it's a battle, why has God let it be that? Why doesn't He take away all the temptation and let us go on in the new way?"

"Because only by overcoming can we build strong characters. God wants us to endure, so that we may be good soldiers in His army. Only those who have had their faith tested and have overcome are the ones who have the greatest faith, for they have proved to themselves what God can do. It's a battle, but it's a glorious one, and after the war is finally over and we are with the Lord, the reward will convince us that it was more than worthwhile. Just to hear the Lord Jesus say, 'Well done, good and faithful servant,' will be enough for me."

Beth's eyes were shining and her face was alight with a glow that made her more attractive than ever.

"I want to be an overcomer," Lisa murmured, "if it gives such joy as you have, for I know that it must be worthwhile. But I don't know how to pray," she confessed.

"I shall pray with you and I know that the Holy Spirit will teach you how to pray. God's Word says that He prays for us while we are praying, because He knows the mind and will of God better than we do."

"All that I know about prayer is what I heard in the synagogue. They were only words and I didn't even want to repeat them."

"When you pray, just talk to God as if you were talking to your father. He's concerned about everything that touches your life. Don't be afraid to pour out your heart to Him. He knows your need and your weakness even before you pray, and He has promised to meet your every need in His way and His time. But be sure when you pray to say 'Thy will be done.' "

"I shall try, but how can I say 'Thy will be done' when I want Paul to be alive?"

Beth put her arm around Lisa and said tenderly, "His will is going to be done whether you're yielded or not, for He knows what is best for you. But to be yielded brings peace and to be rebellious when prayer isn't answered brings unhappiness and will lead you away from the Lord. Suppose we pray together now."

They knelt together and Beth prayed that Lisa would learn to trust and to be yielded to God's will about Paul. She prayed that if it was His will, that she would find him and that they would be happy together, but if it wasn't His will, she would find strength to bear whatever disappointment might come.

When they arose from their knees there were tears streaming down Lisa's face. She threw her arms around Beth and murmured, "I shall try to be yielded and to be and do what God wants, but I know it will be hard. But you said it would be worth it all in the end. I shall try to believe that and to remember it if disappointment and sorrow should come. How I love you!" she added and kissed Beth upon her cheek.

"I love you, my dear, very much. Now let's read that chapter that I was telling you about."

She got out her Bible and began to explain what the Christian armor meant. They didn't realize how long they had been talking until Glen came and found them absorbed in their study.

"Well! If this isn't a fine way for a tired businessman to be treated!" he exclaimed with mock severity. "No dinner, not even the table set while you two sit and gabble."

Lisa jumped to her feet at once. She had forgotten that she was only a hired maid and that it was her task to prepare dinner.

"I'm sorry," she said. "I'll have everything ready in a little while. Everything is ready but the meat and I'll soon have that ready."

"Sit down, Lisa," Beth said. "This tired man can wait. We've had more important things to talk about than to worry about a late dinner. Glen was only joking."

Lisa sat down while Beth told Glen what they had been talking about. Glen's eyes glowed as he heard. He looked at Lisa and he seemed to see a new light in her eyes and a new expression upon her face. The hard light had vanished and the expression of sadness and despair had softened while her smile met his admiring gaze. If only Paul wasn't in the way! Then he reproached himself for that wish. While she was fighting a battle against despair, he must fight his own battle between his desire and her happiness.

The dinner wasn't too late and they all enjoyed it more than any meal they had had together, for there was peace in all their hearts.

A few days later Lotta came to see Beth and Lisa. Lisa had been to the prayer meeting and had publicly confessed her belief in Jesus as her Saviour and friends had crowded around her after the service, while they told her how they had been praying for her.

She saw Lotta in the distance, but the girl didn't come near her. Lisa wished that she could tell Lotta that she had nothing to fear from her, that she wasn't in love with Glen. She was thankful that there was no longer any resentment in her heart for the way she had acted toward her. She had won that small victory and she rejoiced over it.

When Lotta came, her embarrassment was quite evident, though Beth greeted her cordially and tried to make her feel welcome. Lotta turned to Lisa who had stood silently while Beth greeted her and led her into the living room.

"I came to apologize to you, Lisa," Lotta said. "I was terribly rude the last time I was here. I've been ashamed of myself ever since. I wanted to come to you at prayer meeting, but I was afraid you would resent me, so I stayed away. I want to tell you how glad I am that you've accepted Christ as your Saviour. Please forgive me for the way I acted."

"I've already forgiven you," Lisa told her. "It did hurt and I was angry and I hated you, for you seemed just like all the others who called themselves Christians, But I don't hate you any longer and I'm glad I don't."

"I surely didn't act like a Christian," Lotta confessed. "I asked the Lord to forgive me, but I had to ask for your forgiveness, too, before I could feel that I was truly in fellowship with the Lord again."

"I understand why you acted like you did. You were afraid that I would try to take Glen away from you," Lisa told her frankly.

Lotta colored. "I did feel a little jealous," she admitted. "You're so beautiful that I couldn't see how Glen could help loving you, and he is so handsome that I couldn't see how you could help falling in love with him."

"Don't be afraid," Lisa told her. "My heart belongs to someone in my homeland. It will always belong to him."

"I've loved Glen for a long time," Lotta admitted. "We had a sort of engagement before he went away, though there was nothing binding upon either of us, but I'm afraid that he has changed. He surely doesn't feel the same toward me or he would have gotten in touch with me when he first came home."

"The war has changed many of the fellows, dear," Beth said. "Glen has just about recovered his old self. He was weak and dejected when he came home. He had been ill and he felt condemnation over having had to kill so ruthlessly. It took quite some time to get over that. Give him time. I'm sure that the Lord will work it out for good to both of you, for you are His children."

"I shall pray that both of you will be happy together," Lisa told her. Her face glowed. "Doesn't that sound strange, coming from me? But it's wonderful! Wonderful!"

"It really is wonderful," Beth agreed as her loving gaze rested upon Lisa's face.

CHAPTER 19

SUMMER HAD ARRIVED, and Lisa still tried to wait patiently for the long awaited permission that would give her the right to a passport and a return if she decided to return. She had promised Glen that she would return if her mission met with failure. Beth had assured her that she would be welcome to stay with them if she came back, and Lisa felt that she would never be happy elsewhere if she didn't find Paul. She had no plans for her life further than to return to the only ones left to love her, if Paul was not alive.

She was so sure that God would answer her prayer that she should find Paul alive, that she would not think beyond that.

Beth was wondering what would happen to Glen if Lisa should find Paul living. She knew that Glen was unhappy, though he tried to conceal it from her keen eyes. She knew that he was trying to conquer his love for Lisa and that he was hoping, for her sake, that she would find Paul. Her heart ached for him.

Finally one evening Glen came home with the news for which Lisa had been waiting so anxiously. At last the necessary papers had come through and she was free to leave on her search. He tried to be glad and he was, for her sake, but his heart was heavy, for he knew that in a few short days he might be seeing her for the last time, or, if he ever saw her again, she might belong to Paul.

Lisa wept when he gave her the news. She found it almost impossible to believe that, after all this time, she might see Paul again. When she dried her eyes she was able to thank Glen for what he had done. She asked him if he would get the information for her about her passage and the reservations. He promised to do that at once.

She was thankful that she had saved enough to pay for her passage, but both Beth and Glen insisted that she should let them lend her enough to meet any emergency.

When the day came for her departure, Glen insisted upon taking her to the dock. She gave Beth a tearful good-by. Beth didn't want to go to the dock with them. She felt that those last moments belonged to Glen.

"I feel as if I were telling my mother good-by," Lisa told Beth through her tears. "You treated me as if I were a daughter, not a servant. I shall always be grateful and I shall always pray for you."

"I never thought of you as a servant, dear," Beth told her. "You seemed more like a daughter and I love you as if you were one. May the Lord undertake for you and bring you joy."

Then she waved good-by as Lisa got into the car and Glen drove away.

"It will be terribly lonesome there at home without you," he said as they drove along. "Home will never seem the same without you."

"You'll never know how much you and your mother have meant to me," she told him. "It meant a great deal to know that there was someone left in the world who loved me. Perhaps you'll have Lotta with you and then you won't miss me at all."

"I know what Mom has been up to," he said with a faint smile. "She's been trying to prepare me for the time when you would be gone. She knows that I love you, Lisa, and knows how I feel because you can never belong to me. But it just won't work. Lotta is a fine girl, but she's not you. If I can't have you, I don't believe I shall ever want anyone else."

"I hope that isn't true, Glen," she said. "I wish for you every happiness, because you deserve it. If there had never been Paul, I know I could love you in the way you want me to, but he's there and I can't change. Be kind and pray for me, that God will answer my prayer and bring me happiness at the end of my journey."

"I shall do that, but it won't be easy to pray that you'll be happy with someone else when I want you so much for myself. But I do want you to be happy."

When they reached the dock the passengers were already going aboard. Glen went with her as far as he could go, for visitors were already leaving the ship. His face told her what he didn't try to conceal and her heart ached for him. He took her hand and told her good-by while her lips quivered and his eyes filled with tears. He was looking at her as if he were seeing her for the last time. She reached up impulsively and put her arms around his neck, then she kissed him.

"Good-by," he whispered, "and may God bless you and keep you."

"Good-by, Glen, the dearest friend I ever had. I shall always love you and I pray that you may find happiness. How I wish that it could have been different."

She went on board and stood beside the rail waving to him until he was only a blurred dot in the midst of a waving throng. Her eyes were blinded by tears as he finally vanished from her sight.

Glen turned away and made his way back to his car. There were tears in his eyes and he wasn't ashamed of them, but he brushed them away as he started his car and went to his work. He must try to forget. He would keep so busy that there would be no time for thinking, for remembering would only bring added pain and at this moment it seemed more than he could bear.

As the ship sailed out of the harbor, Lisa took a last look at the Statue of Liberty raising the torch of freedom and she thought how different this was from her first glimpse of the statue. How desolate and stricken she had been. Then there had been despair and hopelessness, with nothing to look forward to, no place to go, nothing but darkness and shattered hopes. Now there was peace in her heart and love for those who had been kind. There was thanksgiving for having had such wonderful friends. There was peace and hope where there had been desolation and despair.

She uttered a prayer to God who had brought all this to pass in His infinite mercy. She remembered how she had looked when she had gone to her first job, how ragged and forlorn, with nothing but the clothes she had worn through a part of that long agonizing march. Now she had becoming clothes. Beth had seen to that.

If she should find Paul, she didn't know what his financial condition would be. She knew that there was devastation and poverty everywhere throughout the war-torn countryside. If she and Paul could be married, it might be many months before they could know anything but the direst poverty. But nothing would matter, poverty, sickness, suffering, so long as she and Paul were together.

Those who saw her on deck paused for a second look at her, for the expression of happiness upon her face made it more beautiful than ever and the light in her eyes made them more brilliant and lovely. She soon made friends and the time passed pleasantly until they docked and she was on her way to her home town.

As the train rolled along, she saw the desolation and destruction that lay before her. War had left its terrible mark all along the way. Ruins stood where villages had been. Trees that had once been beautiful, spreading their green branches for shelter, were blackened, witch-like skeletons. There were a few people who had returned and had tried to rebuild ruined homes and lives, but they were living in the midst of ruins which hadn't yet been cleared away.

She wondered what her home town would look like, if the war had passed them by, or if at the very last the bombs had come with their merciless destruction. She longed to know and yet she dreaded to know, the nearer she approached the end of her journey. What would she do if the town had been destroyed and Paul wouldn't be able to wait for her at his home as he had promised? Where could she look for him? How could she ever find out whether or not he was still alive, if he wasn't there? If there was no one there who had known him?

She hadn't thought of all this while she was in America and she was glad that she hadn't, for now she was on the verge of panic. She could scarcely sit calmly in her seat until she reached the place where she would have to change trains.

There was a long layover while she waited for the local train that would pass through her home town. The ride there of an hour or so was spent in an agony of suspense. She longed to ask the conductor about the town, but she was afraid to know. She would put off the moment until she reached the end of her journey and saw the truth herself.

At last the train blew for her station and she got her suitcase and prepared to get off. She stood for a moment looking anxiously about her as the train pulled out of sight. The depot agent came up to take care of her baggage. She told him to hold it until she called for it and he gave her a check and rolled it to the station while she still stood looking about her.

Hope and thanksgiving rose within her. The town hadn't been bombed. The war had mercifully spared it. It was out of the route of the armies during the last invasion and it seemed almost as it had been when she left it. She walked slowly down the street, trying to still the tumult in her heart. Now that she had reached the end of her journey, excitement, hope and fear swept through her and she drew in her breath in little gasps as she walked along.

She passed Greda's home and recognized it and the sight brought back memories of the old days. She wondered if Greda had found someone she could love, if her love for Paul had been forgotten in the love of someone who loved her. She remembered how Greda had tried to hide that love and how jealous she had been of her that night at the party.

Her heart throbbed with a quick stab of pain as she saw the ruins of her home. The charred framework still remained, a huddle of blackened wood and chimneys which stood like mute sentinels among the wreckage. She knew that this must have been the work of the soldiers who took them away that day, for down the street she saw the ruins of another Jewish home.

Then she saw Paul's home. The doors were shut although it was summer and the day was warm. It was almost noon and there were few people on the street and none in her vicinity.

She stood looking at the house, afraid to go in and knock on the door. What if Paul wasn't there? What if strangers now occupied the house? Then she saw that this wasn't the house that had been there when she lived across the street. It had been rebuilt. It was much like the old one, but it was new and smaller.

Now her fears increased. Paul's home must have been burned also when they were taken away, but someone had been able to rebuild after the war ended. Was it Paul or someone else? She was even more afraid to find out the truth. She opened the gate and stood there a moment hesitating. She heard a step behind her and turned. It was Paul.

CHAPTER 20

THEY STOOD A FEW FEET APART, staring at each other
as if they couldn't believe what they saw. Lisa caught
her breath and stood transfixed, waiting for the moment
when she could be released from this sudden paralysis,
and rush into his arms. She saw in that first glance that
he had aged since she had last seen him. He was thinner
and there was a haggard expression upon his face that
could have been caused by the suffering he had endured
in the prison camp. While she stood there she lost count
of time. Joy, unbelievable joy rushed over her with thanksgiving that her search had ended. Paul was here, alive
and well.

She uttered his name in a glad whisper. "Paul! Paul!"
she breathed, then she stood waiting for him to come to her
and take her in his arms.

Something held her back from rushing into his arms,
something which she saw in his eyes, something that she
hadn't noticed before. There was horror there and agony,
no glad light, no glad cry of welcome and of joy that at last
she had returned, while he had been waiting for her
through the years.

At last he found his voice but the cry was one of
despair.

"Lisa! Lisa!" It was a cry of agony.

He didn't hold out his arms to her as she had visioned
so many times. He stood as if he were rooted to the spot
and couldn't even raise his arms.

"Lisa! Lisa!" he moaned in a voice that rose to a wail.

Cold fear engulfed her. Something was terribly wrong.

"You're not glad to see me," she managed to stammer as she watched his face and saw the look of desperation in his eyes.

"Glad! Glad!" he echoed. "I'm glad, yes, but you've come too late! Too late!"

Tears that he seemed unconscious of trickled down his wan face. She moved nearer and looked into his hopeless eyes while a pall of fear and horror swept over her.

What's the matter, Paul?" she asked. "Is this the way to greet me, after I've waited all these years to see you again? Don't you love me any more?"

"Don't I love you any more?" he repeated, gasping out the words. "How could I ever stop loving you? But you've come too late, Lisa. I'm married. Why didn't you come sooner?"

"Married!" she cried, unbelieving. "How could you, Paul, if you still love me? You promised to wait for me. How could you do such a thing? I've waited and suffered through all the long years, just living for the time when I could come back and see if you were alive. I felt that if you were, you would be waiting for me as you promised. How could you do such a thing?"

"Because I was sure you were dead. Hans came back for a little while before the invasion began. He had been wounded and came home for a rest before rejoining the army. He told Greda that you were dead, that you had tried to escape and that you had been shot."

"It didn't take you long to forget me," she said bitterly.

Her heart was torn with such grief that she felt weak and sick.

"I didn't forget you, Lisa. I grieved for you night and day. I couldn't eat and I almost died. I wished that I could die."

"Then you found comfort and forgetfulness in some-one's arms," she said.

"It wasn't like that at all. When I was on my way to the prison camp, I fell by the wayside. I was suffering with my leg and I was exhausted. One of the soldiers was ordered to kill me. He clubbed me and left me for dead. I managed to get back here, but I knew that if they found me, I would be killed. Greda saw me in the early morning when I finally reached home and found that my house had been burned just as yours was. She took me in and took care of me until the war was over."

He paused for a moment, unable to go on with her agonized eyes watching him.

"Then you and Greda got married," she stated while her eyes grew hard and resentful. Greda had won him after all.

He nodded and bowed his head before the scorn in her eyes.

"So while I was waiting and suffering and living only for the time when I should find you, you had forgotten your promise to wait for me."

"I told you that Hans told Greda that you were dead," he said.

"You should have known better than to have believed Hans," she retorted. "I escaped and went to America with other refugees. I met a man who loves me and wants to marry me, but I couldn't think of marrying anyone while I had the love for you in my heart. I could have married him and been happy, if I hadn't been so determined to come back and see whether or not you were still alive. But you found happiness with someone else while I was suffering and waiting."

"Listen to me, Lisa, and don't condemn me, please," he begged. "Greda went out and worked to support me when I couldn't work for myself. She nursed me back to health and she wouldn't let me die when I wanted to die after I believed you were dead. During the last winter of the war, her parents died within weeks of each other, and we were alone. When I took her in my arms and tried to comfort her, she told me how much she loved me. I cared for her in a way because she had been so good to me, so I asked her to marry me. There seemed nothing else to do, for I still had to stay hidden in the house until Hitler's forces were conquered. I thought that if I could make her happy, it was the least I could do, for there was nothing left for me in life. Everyone I loved was dead. I have made her happy, but she doesn't know how I have suffered, knowing that you were dead and that I'd never see you again. She has been a good wife to me and I was glad that we had married. Glad until now." His voice ended in a moan.

She gazed at him for a long moment, while she fought back the tears, then she turned away.

"Wait!" he cried. "Don't go, Lisa. Don't leave me! Come inside and see Greda. She's been ill and she's still in bed. That's why I came home, to see if she needed anything."

"Why should I want to see her?" Lisa exclaimed. "And why should I stay? You have her. Make her happy if you can."

"Where are you going?" he asked in tones of despair.

"Back to America and to those who love me," she replied. "I never want to see you or this place again. I hope I can forget that I ever knew you."

He ran to her and took her in his arms while she struggled to release herself.

"I can't let you go! I can't!" he cried as he held her.

He bent and kissed her and for one brief moment her lips answered his clinging caress, then she pushed him from her and said in a voice choked with sobs, "I don't want your kisses. They belong to her. Go on inside and continue to pay your debt to her. I hope I never see you again."

She went slowly down the street toward the depot while he watched her through misery-filled eyes, then he turned and went into the house.

He found Greda much worse. Her eyes were bright with fever and her breath came in labored gasps. He thought dully that he'd have to go for the doctor. What had seemed like a bad cold appeared to be something more serious.

"Where have you been so long?" she asked as she gasped for breath. "I thought I heard you talking to someone. Who was it?"

He stared at her dully. "It was Lisa. She came back looking for me."

"Lisa! Lisa!" she cried. "But I thought Hans said she was dead."

Something in her eyes and in her voice gave him a sudden thought. She couldn't meet his eyes, but turned her face away.

"Did Hans tell you that Lisa was dead?" he probed.

Suspicion assailed him. He didn't remember having heard her mention talking to Hans until long after he had left, until he had told her that he would never stop waiting for Lisa. It was then that she had told him what Hans had said.

She waited a long time before she answered.

"No — he — didn't," she stammered. "But I thought that surely she must be dead, for it had been so long since she had been taken to the concentration camp and the others had either been released or killed."

"Then you lied to me and I've been grieving for her all this time when she was living with the hope of coming back here and finding me waiting for her." His voice was accusing.

"It was because I loved you so much," she confessed. "I knew that you would never marry me if you thought she might be alive. Please don't be angry with me, Paul," she begged as he turned away and clenched his fists while he tried to control his anger and the despair which assailed him.

He turned upon her fiercely. "Do you know what you've done?" he stormed. "You've wrecked two lives and you've destroyed all the pity and gratitude I felt toward you. I shall do all I can to repay my debt to you, but I shall hate you every minute of my life."

He went for the doctor while she hid her face in the pillow and wept.

Paul started to the depot on his way to the doctor. He knew that Lisa would be there waiting for the afternoon train, but when he had gone only a little way, he turned back and continued on his way. What was the use of seeing her again? What good would it do to prolong the agony? He regretted his angry words to Greda, but bitterness and despair rankled within him. When he thought of the days ahead when he must live with the wife he had never loved, knowing what she had done by her falsehood, he didn't think he could endure it. But when he remembered her devotion to him and the risk she had taken in keeping him hidden all those long months, he knew that he would spend the rest of his heartbroken life in trying to repay her for what she had done. He wished now that he had died on the roadside. Then he wouldn't have lived to see this day.

that she had been hungry without realizing it and she felt more calm.

"Your room is ready for you," Beth told her. "It has looked forlorn without you. Just be assured that this is your home and that you belong to us."

"You're wonderful!" Lisa exclaimed as tears again filled her eyes. "What would I have done without you? I'll work for you as I did, but I won't accept any wages. If I'm a part of the family, then treat me like one and don't offer to pay me. I have no further need for money now." Her lip trembled.

"Let's not talk about that tonight. Just sleep and even in your dreams remember that we love you and that Another greater than us also loves you. You can never get away from His love. Let's have a word of prayer before we go."

Glen had slipped a record on the phonograph and as Beth prayed the lovely song rang out softly as the background of her prayer. Lisa was not listening to the prayer, but sat there with eyes open and fixed before her, for she rebelled against the prayer. But she couldn't fail to hear the words of the song, "Heartaches, take them all to Jesus. He will take your heartaches all away."

Was that true? How could it be? She couldn't believe it, for she knew that she would carry her heartache for the rest of her life. Tonight she had no desire to take anything to Jesus. She was stubbornly trying to carry her heartache all alone in her own strength, a strength which was only weakness.

Tears trickled down her face as she slipped from the couch and went to her room.

"Poor kid!" Glen remarked when they rose from their knees and saw that she had disappeared. "She's going to have a rough road to travel for a while. I pray that she'll be willing to look to the Lord to help her."

"She will, for we shall pray, and I know that the Lord will answer and give her what is best for her," Beth asserted.

"I wonder if God wants me to have her," Glen mused

aloud. "I love her so much, yet I wonder if it will be His will for her to love me."

"I've wondered that myself, son," Beth told him. "I want to see you happy and I want you to have her, if that is what God wants, but I somehow have a feeling that it may never be. I shall pray that you will be guided by His will and that neither of you will be hurt through this love you have for her."

"That's a strange thing for you to say, Mom."

"I know, but that's the way I feel. Let's do all we can to make her happy and let's pray that she may recover the faith that she had. She's a babe in Christ and this is her first great test. I'll admit that it is a severe one, but God knows what He's doing and I know that everything will work out for the best in the end."

"I'll join you in prayer, but I shall throw in a little petition of my own, which I hope that He will answer."

"If it is His will, don't forget that," Beth advised as she went to her room.

"I'll remember to say that," he promised as she left him.

He sat there for quite a while thinking, before he settled down to studying for the examination which was due in a few days. He murmured, "If it is Thy will, Father," then he went to the desk and opened his book. He tried to study, but Lisa's tear-drenched eyes stood between him and the printed page and after a time he gave up and went to his room, deciding to get up early and study before breakfast.

In her room Lisa lay wide-eyed in the darkness. It was the first time she had gone to bed in this room without praying after she had accepted Christ as her Saviour, and there was a sense of guilt within her as she got into bed without that prayer.

She hadn't prayed since she left Paul, but there was an emptiness in her heart, now that she was back in the familiar surroundings, which brought a sense of guilt and a new pain. As she finally slept, there rang like an echo through her slumber, the words of the song. "Heartaches, take them all to Jesus. He will take your heartaches all away." She wanted to believe. It was the first time she had wanted to since that last look she had had of Paul. But just now she couldn't.

CHAPTER 22

LISA FOUND IT DIFFICULT to adjust to this new phase of her life. Before, there had been the compelling driving force which kept her going, when hope had been the mainspring of her life, but now that the hope was no longer there, she had no desire to take up life without that hope. She was moody and listless, helping Beth with her work as if nothing had changed, but taking no interest in anything that Beth tried to do to interest her.

Beth was tactful and sympathetic and she didn't reproach Lisa for her moodiness. She knew how the girl was suffering and she knew that only the Lord could change her attitude toward life and toward Him. She was cheerful in her conversation and tried to show in many little ways her love for Lisa and that she understood and sympathized with her. She knew that if Paul had been dead it would have been easier for her to overcome her grief, but this was a living heartache which was ever with her and she didn't even try to overcome it.

Beth didn't ask her to go with her to church, but one Sunday she turned on the phonograph and suggested that Lisa would find some interesting book on the table.

Lisa listened rather disinterestedly for a while to the music but presently she listened with keener interest. She realized that Beth had had a method in her selection of the records. She didn't resent it, for her heart was touched by the songs, and they seemed to meet her need.

Tears came to her eyes as she heard a beautiful soprano singing "The Ninety and Nine." It seemed that she must be that one lost sheep. She knew that she had strayed away from the place where she should be in the love of God. The last song seemed to be sent from God. She listened with rapt attention while her heart melted and the tears came. The words rang out like a call from the Saviour whom she had once loved and toward whom she had been so rebellious, "Softly and tenderly Jesus is calling." Then the chorus, "Come home, come home, ye who are weary come home."

She was weary, utterly weary, so weary that she wanted to die, but she knew that dying wasn't the remedy. She must come home to the Father's love and to the arms of the Shepherd.

She knelt beside the couch and poured out her grief and begged for forgiveness and mercy. She prayed for strength to trust and to make something worthwhile of her life and to overcome the heartache, so that she might live a life of service even in the face of sorrow and disappointment.

Peace came to her heart once more, peace that she had thought gone forever and when Beth came home, she found Lisa with a different light in her eyes and a smile upon her lips. She silently thanked the Lord for answered prayer, for she knew that something had happened to change her.

"Thanks for putting those records on for me," Lisa said. "The Lord has forgiven me for all of my sin of doubt and bitterness and I know that I'll never doubt His love again."

"Thank the Lord that He has answered prayer," Beth murmured while tears filled her eyes. "He is gracious and merciful to both of us."

Glen came in later from taking Lotta home. When he saw Lisa he knew that something wonderful had happened to her, though he didn't comment upon it. They went into the kitchen together while Lisa warmed the dinner and Beth set the table. Glen chattered away, hoping that Lisa would respond to his cheerfulness and she did. They were soon talking and laughing happily as Lisa put the food on the table and they took their places.

"May I return thanks?" Lisa asked.

"Of course, dear," Beth told her while Glen stared wide-eyed. It was the first time she had asked such a thing.

Lisa repeated the words she had often heard Glen speak, then she thanked the Lord for what He had done for her and for the peace that she had in her heart as her faith had been restored.

Glen uttered a solemn amen when she had finished. He gave her a warm smile as their eyes met and then Lisa told him what had happened.

"I shall let bygones be bygones," she told him. "What is past was the Lord's doing and I shall be obedient to His will. I won't worry about the future, because I know that it is in His hands. That doesn't mean that I can forget, but I won't be bitter any longer."

Glen was overjoyed at the way things were working out. He forgot his gloomy uncertainty and his mother's more gloomy words about Lisa, and his love grew as the days passed. He was willing to wait for time to heal the wound, hoping and praying that she would learn to love him.

The weeks passed more rapidly than Lisa realized until it was almost a year since she had returned. One evening she and Glen were sitting alone in the living room while Beth had gone visiting.

Glen turned to Lisa in a brief silence and said, "Lisa, I've tried to wait patiently while I hoped that you would learn to love me, but I can't wait any longer. Could you care for me even a little? I love you so much. Will you marry me? I'll try to make you happy. You would make me the happiest man in the world if you'd only say yes."

She looked at him sadly. "I wish I could say yes, Glen, but if I told you that I loved you, it wouldn't be the truth. Love seems to be dead within me. I've loved Paul for so long that there doesn't seem to be any room for any other love in my heart. It wouldn't be fair for me to say yes, I'll marry you, if I can't give you the love you ask for. I couldn't make you happy and both of us would be miserable with that kind of marriage."

"I love you enough to marry you even though you don't have that kind of love for me," he insisted. "I believe that we could have a happy congenial life together and that one day you might be able to give me the kind of love I crave, if you'd only say you will."

She waited a long moment before she answered, while he took her hands and held them in his firm grasp. The temptation was strong to tell him that she would marry him. It was true that he could make her happy. There would be peace and protection as his wife and she would be happy to know that he loved her. It would be a comfort after all the storm and suffering. But would it be fair to him for her to marry him without that love to which he was entitled? She would be cheating him and in time he might grow bitter himself when he realized how empty his life was without the love he deserved.

"Give me time, Glen," she begged. "Give me time to think it over. I do want to love you. Perhaps some day I shall, for you are wonderful and I know you'd make me happy. But I don't want to cheat you. Perhaps some day you would find someone else you could love and who would love you. Then you would have what you deserve."

"But I want you," he persisted. "I don't want anyone else. I'll never love anyone else."

"What about Lotta? She loves you. Her heart must ache like mine has to know that I have taken her place."

"Let's not talk about her, let's talk about you. Please say yes."

"Give me time, please. I want to be fair to you. There's no hurry. I'm not going to run away." Her face contracted with pain for a moment, but she managed to smile.

"How long do I have to wait?" he asked.

"Just a little while. Until I'm sure that it's the right thing to do."

He drew her to him and she didn't resist. He held her in his arms for a moment, then kissed her gently. She felt the warmth of his love as her lips met his and in the shelter of his arms against his throbbing heart, she thought that perhaps she would do the right thing to say yes. But the memory of Paul came to her and she withdrew from Glen's arms while sadness crept into her eyes. She knew that there never could be another and she knew that she could never give Glen the answer he longed for.

She couldn't tell him now, yet she hated to keep him hoping when she knew that his hope would never be realized. She wondered what she should do and when she should tell him.

Glen was happy in hope and he felt that his happiness would soon be complete. He was busy with his final examinations in his law course and he couldn't spend much time at home. Lisa was glad, for it gave her a respite. The weeks slipped by and her world seemed at peace, though she knew that it would lose its peace when she had to tell Glen the truth. She would suffer with him, but it was better that it should be now than to have more suffering later on.

One evening she was alone. Beth had gone to a meeting and Glen was at the office. She was reading when the bell rang. She went to the door and opened it. Paul was standing there as if he were a ghost out of the past.

She uttered a little cry and stood there transfixed.

He smiled at her and said, "May I come in?"

"Paul!" she exclaimed as she let him in and closed the door. "Why have you come here?"

"I came to find you," he told her. "I hope I'm not too late. I hope you're not married to someone else."

She sat down and he sat nearby while she stared at him solemnly.

"What difference should that make to you," she asked, "since you're married yourself?"

"I'm not married any longer," he said as a shadow crossed his face. "Greda died just a few weeks after you were there. What I thought was a bad cold proved to be TB in its fastest form. She had a hemorrhage and died just after the doctor got there."

"I'm sorry," she said mechanically.

"I reproached myself for what I said to her after you left and I apologized to her. She said she deserved everything I had said. She confessed that she had lied to me when she said that Hans had told her you had been killed. She thought you must have died, so she told me that, hoping that I would marry her if I knew you were dead. After I told her what I did, I don't think she wanted to live. I was sorry if I had hurt her, but after she died, I had to find you, Lisa, so I left as soon as I could sell my house and get my affairs straightened out and get a passport."

"How did you find me?" she asked.

She was so shocked by his appearance that she couldn't feel any emotion. She didn't even know whether she was glad or sorry. She noticed how he had aged since she had last seen him, but he still seemed to her as handsome as the day she had first been held in his arms.

"I had no idea how I should find you, but I knew that if I could just get to America, I would spend the rest of my life, if necessary, looking for you. There was a chaplain from the army on board the ship. We got to be friends and I told him my problem. It wasn't too difficult for him to find where you lived. He got the information from the immigration service where you got your passport to Germany. I was fortunate to have him do the work for me, for I might not ever have found you without his help. I was so afraid that you would be married to someone else before I could find you."

"Perhaps then you would have known how I felt when I knew that you had married someone else," she said with a trace of bitterness.

The wound was still there, though she had told herself that it had been healed.

"That was cruel, Lisa. I told you why I married Greda. I never stopped loving you. Do you still hate me? If you knew how I suffered when I was trying to make Greda happy, you wouldn't reproach me. I'm sure she knew that I never loved her, though I did try to make her believe that I did. There never could be another but you. Have you forgotten the love you once had for me, Lisa? You're all I have to live for. Say you don't hate me."

He held out his arms to her and his eyes were pleading. She looked into those eyes which she had seen so often in her dreams, and everything that was past, the suffering and the bitterness, the struggle to forget, were all swept away in the love which had been in her heart all through the years. With a little cry she went to him and was held in his arms. Their lips met in a kiss that opened once more to her heart the floodgates of happiness which she never hoped to have again.

The door opened and Beth stood staring at them with wide, amazed eyes. When they became conscious of her presence, Lisa released herself from Paul's arms.

"This is Paul," she said simply. "His wife has died and he has come for me."

After Lisa had explained to Beth, Paul turned to go. He was glad that he had studied English, but he had forgotten some of it and the words came slowly and haltingly.

"I have a place in the city," he said. "I'll come back again tomorrow."

After he left, the two women stood for a while just looking at each other, then Lisa began to weep silently.

"I'm sorry that it didn't turn out the way you wanted," she said. "I did want to make Glen happy, but I just couldn't forget Paul, even though I was so angry with him for marrying Greda. Please don't be angry with me, because I can't help loving Paul."

"I'm not angry, my dear," Beth assured her. "I do feel sorry for Glen because I know how this will hurt him, but if you couldn't love him, it's best that it ended this way. Just remember that I shall always love you and pray for your happiness."

"How good you are to me," Lisa murmured as she dried her eyes, gave Beth a timid kiss and went to her room.

As Beth went to her room, there were tears in her eyes. They were for Glen, for she knew how he would feel when she told him the news.

CHAPTER 23

BETH DREADED TELLING GLEN, for she knew what a shock it would be, but she had confidence in his strength and in his reliance upon God to carry him through any testing.

When she told him, his face went white and she was frightened, but he recovered himself after a struggle to regain his composure, and said as calmly as he could, "If this is the will of God, what can I do but submit? I have prayed, 'Thy will be done.'"

His voice broke and he covered his face with his hands. Beth put her arms around him and wept silently for him while he gained control of himself.

"Remember that you said you wondered if Lisa would ever belong to you?" she said. "And that I said I had that same question in my heart?"

He nodded. "She was honest with me. She told me that she was afraid that she never could give me the kind of love I asked for. I wanted her to marry me anyway, but she begged for time. How glad I am that she made me wait! It would have been such a tragedy if we had married and he should have come afterwards. All three of our lives would have been wrecked."

"I pray that yours won't be wrecked, son," Beth said.

"Don't worry, Mother, it won't. It is a blow and I may never recover from it, but I'll never let it get me down. I still know where my strength lies and I know that God will see me through."

Lisa dreaded meeting Glen the next morning, but he greeted her with a smile and seemed as cheerful as if nothing had happened.

157

Before he left, she had a few moments with him alone. "I wish I knew what to say," she told him. "You know that I was honest with you when I asked you to wait. I tried to love you, but I couldn't forget that I still loved Paul. You won't blame either of us for what has happened, will you? You know that I never dreamed that this would happen."

"How could I blame you?" he said simply. "Just be happy and forget me."

"I could never do that," she said emphatically. "I shall pray for your happiness."

He left her abruptly, for he didn't want her to see the suffering which he felt must show upon his face and in his eyes.

"I feel that I should leave," Lisa told Beth. "I'll look for some place where I can get a job until Paul can find work. I feel like an ingrate, but I feel that it would be best for all of us if I should go."

"You're welcome to remain here until you make other plans," Beth assured her. "There's one thing that worries me though. Paul isn't a Christian and you are."

"I've thought of that," Lisa said. "I'll try to win him before we are married. It may be hard, but I've had hard things to cope with before now. I'm sure he can't be as hard to convince as I was. I'll be willing to wait."

She spoke to Paul about it when he came again.

"I've heard it all before," he told her. "That chaplain made me understand and believe that Jesus is our Messiah and he made me want to be the kind of a Christian he was. We spent all of our time together. I didn't have a chance to tell you about it and I've wondered what I should do about it, for I thought that you were still an unbeliever and that you even doubted the existence of God."

"Then have you really accepted Christ as your Saviour?" she asked, thrilled and excited.

"Not yet, but I want to," he replied. "Mr. Archer lives in New York and he has promised to tell me more about what he believes. I want to know more about Jesus

and I know that it will be much easier for me to believe,
now that I know you believe. I'm to meet him tomorrow
night. I'm looking forward to having another talk with
him."

"How wonderful the Lord is!" Lisa exclaimed happily.

"I have some more good news," he told her. "Mr.
Archer knows a man who has a shop in the city and he's
promised me a job if I can qualify. I'm to start to work
tomorrow and see if I can hold the job. I'm sure I can, for
it's the kind of work I did back home. So it may not be
long before our dream will come true and we can have
the home here in America that we talked about so long ago."

"But we never could have dreamed that we would be
called upon to endure so much suffering before that dream
came true," she said with a note of sadness in her voice.
"It just proves that God knows the end from the beginning
and that He gives us strength to bear whatever may come,
if we trust in Him to give us strength. It proves that all
things work together for good to those who love the
Lord. I love Him more tonight than I ever did, for He has
brought you back to me again."

"I've heard Mr. Archer repeat those same words,"
Paul said.

"Just believe and accept the Lord and then everything
will be perfect," she whispered.

"I feel like the man to whom Jesus said, 'Thou art not
far from the kingdom of God,'" Paul remarked reverently.
"I know it won't be long before I enter in."

"Then we shall both go on in the light that He has
given us and then, no matter what happens, we shall be
safe in His love."

"And in our love," he whispered as he took her in his
arms and kissed her.